Island Secrets

by

A. Gardner Strong

Photo by Michael Leonard

First published by Dog Ear Publishing
4010 W. 86th Street, Ste H
Indianapolis, IN 46268
www.dogearpublishing.net

ISBN: 978-1-4575-1109-7

This book is printed on acid-free paper.

This is a work of fiction. Names, characters, places, and incidents are either the product of the author's imagination or used fictitiously, and any resemblance to actual persons, living or dead, events, or locales is entirely coincidental.

Printed in the United States of America

Island Secrets

by

A. Gardner Strong

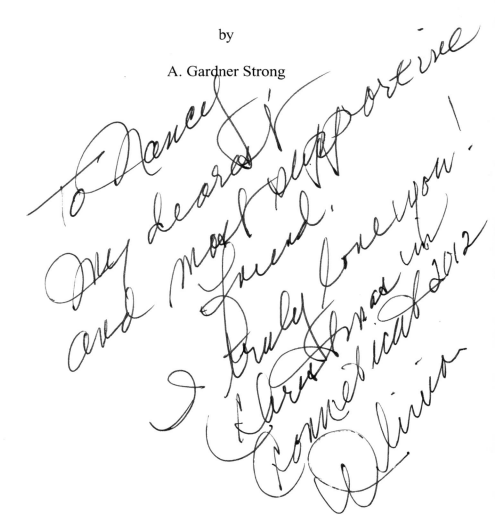

for Chris

Prologue

There was no dispute about it. It had been a perfectly glorious but otherwise unremarkable Summer day on the little island, twelve miles off the coast of Maine. All was as expected. Conditions were perfect. The slight ocean breezes had ushered in a delightfully temperate morning, welcomed by the chirping birds and other venerable early risers, eager to get a jump on the work of the day. In an entirely predictable pattern, the moorings in the harbors were full to capacity, the sleek masts of the seasonal fleet towering over the rugged fishing trawlers, rigged and ready to capitalize on the abundant lobster population throughout the bay.

The locals went about their business as on any other day. Rugged islanders who took their livelihood from the sea had passed through the village landing, coming from and going to their respective boats, their battered waders rolled down, the sleeves of their flannel shirts rolled up. Their faces and necks were all deeply tanned and branded with lines, well earned. Their emotions were matter of fact and hard to read, set, as they were, in various states of either hoping for or feeling satisfaction from a good haul, knowing the elements could change their fortunes without warning or remorse.

Hiram Brown, his seventy-five year old frame stooped by his many years of hard labor trying to eek out a living from the land, had early in the day unloaded a fresh supply of lettuce, peas, green beans, beets, and corn at Waterman's, and had taken the empty crates away in the back of his 1941 Chevy pick-up. His private customers would come to him at the farm, up the long dirt driveway, later in the afternoon. The food tasted better, they maintained, when they got it directly from his weather-beaten hands.

By mid-morning, the tiny village had been overrun by a handsome assortment of Summer people, strolling about with heads held high, wearing their entitlement like the latest fashion from L.L. Bean. The seasonal residents, of course, generally enjoyed a more leisurely pace than the locals, even those who had gotten up early to challenge the nine holes at what passed for a golf club, a mile or so past the village, tucked in the trees along the Eastern coastline. A few weary souls had spent the morning in deep slumber, having stayed up into the wee hours of the morning to hear the youthful senator from Massachusetts, John F. Kennedy, give a stirring acceptance speech at the Democratic National Convention in Los Angeles.

As the dinner hour rolled around, most of the Summer residents gathered with family and friends at the well appointed tables in their private residences, or at the seasonal Casino restaurant in the Village, for an evening of fine food and conversation. The locals, functioning on a slightly different schedule, had taken supper earlier and were now finishing up chores, serving the Summer residents, or casting off to tend their lines and traps. Children of all ages were enthusiastically enjoying many simple pleasures in the remaining daylight, as only the carefree and young at heart can do. Some spent the evening skipping stones off the rocky beach at Mullen's Head, or biking slowly up the long hill on the South Shore Road, over and over, with the single-mindedness of a resolute skier, determined to catch the wind on the exhilarating downhill run.

As dusk approached, the ordinary beauty of the day suddenly disappeared, with no forewarning, and the cloudless sky was replaced by a rare and truly magnificent display of color and light. Conditions could not have been more perfect at that moment for viewing the Aurora Borealis from the island, and the small mass of land thus appeared to be completely enveloped by waves of green and red and blue and yellow, mingling in diffuse patterns, flowing in an upward motion. Witnesses to this unexpected event were struck by the stunning impression that the world had virtually disappeared and the island was floating freely in a rippling sea of colorful light.

Youthful, impressionable minds found the unexpected phenomenon both terrifying and, at the same time, awe inspiring. A fleeting but memorable experience to be sure, those who were fortunate enough to be outside to witness the Northern Lights were, on the whole, struck by the profound beauty, but even more so by the shear magnitude of the display.

Hiram Brown was in his garden, picking peas for his morning delivery. At the onset, he looked up momentarily to assess the unusual patterns in the sky, then, with matter-of-fact determination, bent back toward the ground, bound to complete his task before he lost the light entirely. He stopped only once more, pausing to look over at the gardens to the West of his mother's old place, surprised when he heard the shouting and strange, frightened sounds echoing across the water. He watched for a moment or two then went back to work with myopic zeal, intent upon pushing his troubled thoughts aside.

Overall, the phenomenon lasted less than ten minutes, after which most observers quickly went back to whatever they had been doing. Some islanders were left with the feeling that they had somehow been temporarily propelled into a strange Twilight zone. A few never quite returned...

This is their story.

One

November 22, 2006

N ew Englanders love their region because of the magnificent coastline, majestic mountains, educational and cultural opportunities, fresh lobster, the Boston Red Sox, and the four definitive seasons. Of course, there is nothing written in stone when it comes to New England weather, and odds makers are never, ever safe when predicting an early Spring or a long, blustery Winter. It is New England, after all, and it has long been held that if you don't like the weather, just wait and it will change.

This year, Fall had been remarkably warm, especially along the coast. Although it was late November, when the vast majority of leaves had long ago transitioned into colorful compost material, and families everywhere were busy getting ready for their respective Thanksgiving gatherings, it was hard to avoid the fact that it felt more like a beautiful late September day.

As the early evening hour gave way to the brilliant display of the setting sun, health conscious walkers and nature lovers strolled along the sands of Horseneck Beach. A couple visiting from the mid-West, seeing the ocean for the first time, stood at the edge of Buzzards Bay, smiling in awe as the waves rolled in, reaching for their toes. They jumped back, giggling like school children, as the waters receded quickly to gather momentum for another assault.

Many of the resident seagulls glided in wide, even circles, searching for something worth snatching up for dinner, while others sat atop the dunes, facing into the breeze, conserving their energy as they watched intently. By local statute, dogs were banned from the beach, but, as usual, several dogs and their owners ran along the glittering coastline, leaving their foot and paw prints in the sand, just out of reach of the rising tide.

Away from the shoreline, on the other side of the dunes, a narrow two-lane roadway hugged the edge of the beach. Large boulders were set strategically along the transition from pavement to sand, apparently in an attempt to separate the precious granular particles from the passing cars and trucks in as esthetically pleasing a way as possible.

State police were in charge of keeping order at the beach every Summer, when their mounted unit was a popular sight for most sunbathers. Adults and children always took notice whenever the horses passed by, gracefully slapping at the sand flies with their long brown tails as they patrolled the dunes, looking for mischief makers in the secluded pockets created by the lofty mounds of sand.

It was well known that the troopers generally did a good job keeping the speed along Beach Road under control in the Summer months, but off season, with the barracks empty, the threat of a speeding ticket carried little weight, if any.

On this particular evening, the distinctive sound of a sports car engine grew steadily louder, disrupting the still beauty, and causing several birds resting in the dunes to finally take wing. A vintage silver Jaguar roared into view, gaining speed with each passing second. It was great good fortune that there were no other cars on that stretch of road at that time, or the seagulls would not have been the only witnesses unnerved by the approaching vehicle.

Suddenly, the Jaguar failed to hold the road as it entered a curve. The silver vessel rammed into a boulder, crushing the passenger side of the little car, then flipped up and over, sailing forward with tremendous momentum, about fifty yards beyond the initial site of the crash.

The seagulls that witnessed the crash took off quickly, having no interest in being a part of such an unseemly disruption. A lone dog and his owner, running toward the setting sun, paused and looked around as the first sound of metal on rock caught their attention, but stopped completely and ran toward the roadway when the sound of the exploding car engine filled the air.

~

Night had fallen quickly, as if closing the curtain on this most unfortunate act of foolishness. Before long, flashing strobe lights filled the air as the local police and state troopers tried to secure the crash site. Two ambulances stood by as EMTs hovered around the mangled remains of the silver Jaguar.

The woman was dead. About that there was no doubt. Before long, a grim team from the Bristol County Coroner's office was rolling out a stretcher with a body bag, ready to load it into the back of their van.

The man, obviously the driver, was unconscious, but alive. A group of EMTs quickly stabilized him and lifted him into a waiting ambulance, strapped down to a stretcher, attached to an IV fluid bag, with an oxygen mask covering much of his battered face.

A light rain began to fall, giving a renewed sense of urgency to the State accident reconstruction team, determined to put all the puzzle pieces in place before any scrap of information could be washed away by nature.

Meanwhile, a lone police officer was taking a statement from the beach runner who had called 911, as the dog wagged his tail in excitement, clearly enjoying being in the center of all the activity, blissfully unaware of the grave nature of the event.

~

Peter Winslow had arrived back from New York at his usual time and had been surprised to find a dark, empty home. Puzzled, he had phoned Claire on her cell phone, but she had not answered. Ten minutes later, he tried again and had been surprised to have the phone answered by a deep male voice.

"Oh… I'm sorry… I must have misdialed…" he had said with great perplexity, knowing he had used the speed dial on his own cell phone.

"Wait!" had come the urgent response. "Is this Mr. Winslow?"

~

In New Haven, Connecticut, the moon was looming large over the stately buildings of Yale that have dominated the landscape since the eighteenth century. While there were many students walking about town, alone and in small groups, throughout the campus and along the streets of New Haven, they numbered considerably fewer than normal, many students having departed campus early trying to beat the Thanksgiving rush.

Darkness had settled over the campus, but the many lights that twinkled in the apartment buildings, dorms, shops, and restaurants, and the patrons coming and going, assured New Haven that it would not be entirely deserted over the holiday.

The Book Trader Cafe, a popular hangout on Chapel Street, was busy as ever, serving their fabulous gourmet sandwiches and coffee amid the shelves of good used books. A smiling twenty-eight year old David Winslow, a third generation Yale man, finishing up his formal education and planning, ultimately, to follow his late paternal grandfather into politics, sat at a table by the windows. Next to him was his fiancée, twenty-six year old Anne Holman, and two of their friends, Adam Singer and Nina Cole, sat opposite the couple. It was a casual dinner, with coffee, salads, and generously proportioned gourmet sandwiches covering the table, leaving little room to spare.

"Oh... I'm sorry! It sounds like fun," Anne said, her tone one of exaggerated sadness, "but I have to finish a paper for Professor Ives, *plus* we're leaving really *early* in the morning..."

"My sister's arriving on a red eye from Paris," David said, by way of explanation, "so we were 'volunteered' by my mother to collect her at Logan."

Nina shrugged. "Why don't you have her take the Logan Express so you don't have to drive all the way through Boston?" she suggested. "You wouldn't have to leave so early."

Adam shook his head. "Just tell her to take the bus all the way to Providence!"

David laughed. "You obviously don't know my mother!"

"I know:" Adam said, nodding his head and raising his hands in exaggerated mock protest, "Mothers *live* for Thanksgiving! It's the one holiday that they truly get to call all the shots!"

Nina nodded her agreement. "The command performance!" she pronounced, her eyes wide and expressive.

"Sounds like you've been *summoned* home against your will!" Anne said laughing.

Nina made a face. "You can't imagine how I hate these Thanksgiving gatherings!" She paused for an animated shiver, making sure her point was well taken. "I have *nothing* in common with those people!" she complained. "I mean, engaging in *small* talk with relatives that I *barely* know is *such a waste of time*! My mother denies it, but I swear I must have been adopted!" She leaned in dramatically, as if she were about to say something confidential. "And I don't even *like* turkey!" she hissed. "It would be a *total* waste of time if it wasn't for the stuffing and apple pie!" she concluded as she leaned back from the table.

David laughed and shook his head. "Well, it wouldn't matter if it was Thanksgiving or not! My mother *always* expects me to do "the right thing" – so we're driving to Logan!"

"Hey!" Adam exclaimed, a gleam in his eyes. "That could be a *great* campaign slogan!" He focused on David. "When you run for President, I'll be your campaign manager, O.K.?"

"And your qualifications would be exactly what?" David laughed.

"No, listen!" Adam insisted. "I'm serious! Your mother – *with* all her little common-sense rules — would be a *wonderful* spokesperson!" He smiled broadly and looked to Anne and Nina for validation, then back at David. "I mean, who could *resist* a guy who was raised to be so responsible — and by such a credible woman? Your dad too! They would really make a great impression!"

"You plan to tap my mother for her pearls of wisdom?" David asked with a laugh. "*This* is your *concept* for a winning campaign to get me into the White House?"

An unidentifiable burst of music suddenly rose up from David's pocket, and he reached in to pull out his cell phone. "Sorry! I forgot to put it on vibrate," he said apologetically as he looked at phone display before flipping it open. "Hi, Dad!" he answered with a broad smile, which quickly dissolved into a stunned expression. "*What*?" he asked, his face scrunched as if in an effort to comprehend.

Anne leaned closer, a concerned look on her face, and whispered, "What is it?"

David shook his head. *"What happened?"*

~

Several local news media trucks, apparently alerted to the situation by diligent monitoring of their emergency scanners, were parked just beyond the perimeter set up by the police, satellite dishes extended, lights on, and generators humming.   Three Providence based reporters were broadcasting live, glad that the accident had happened in time to make the ten o'clock news.

Peter Winslow hurriedly parked his car by the Channel 10 truck, then got out and walked in stunned silence toward the nearest police officer, picking up pieces of the news reports as he passed by.

"...There were no eyewitnesses, but speed appears to be a factor. Early indications are that the car continued to be propelled forward about fifty yards from the initial point of impact..."

"...killing the fifty-nine year old female passenger from Westport ..."

"...the forty-five year old male driver from Maine is being taken to the hospital, alive but apparently in critical condition..."

"... Names are being withheld pending notification of next of kin..."

He reached the police officer as if in a trance. "I'm Peter Winslow..." he announced, his voice shaking.

"Yes, sir, Mr. Winslow! Let me get Chief Macomber for

you, sir..." The officer moved away quickly as Peter stood there, dazed by the flashing lights, praying they were somehow all mistaken.

In keeping with New England tradition, the rain had stopped just as suddenly as it had begun, leaving the accident scene lit up in an ethereal mist against a backdrop of moonlit sand, the waves glistening as they rolled in toward the shoreline.

Two

November 25, 2006

It was a beautiful, unseasonably warm November morning when Claire Winthrop Winslow was laid to rest, her sleek mahogany coffin surrounded by a copious assortment of magnificent floral arrangements, the rich colors fusing to create a splendid display, enhanced further by the brilliance of the clear blue sky. Thanks to the lingering mild weather conditions, the grass had retained its deep green color, and a few Autumn leaves continued to cling to the trees along the perimeter of the modest cemetery and scattered among the graves. The throng of mourners filled the designated graveside area, overflowing into the street, which had been cordoned off for the somber occasion. Due to the unseasonable warmth of the day, the women were wearing light weight coats, most casually left unbuttoned, and the men, by and large, wore no overcoats at all.

The immediate family was gathered under a funeral canopy, to the side of the open grave. Peter Winslow, looking every one of his sixty-two years, was seated next to his emotional twenty-one year old daughter, Amelia "Amie" Winslow, a comforting arm around her shoulders. A stoic David Winslow, standing straight and blinking back tears, held the hand of his fiancée, Anne Holman, as tears streamed down her face. Beside them, a muscular male attendant stood next to a fragile looking ninety-two year old Randolph Carver Winthrop, sitting in a wheelchair, a scarf around his neck, and a heavy wool coat buttoned up to keep him warm.

"...We ask you, oh Lord, to accept your humble servant, Claire Winthrop Winslow, so cruelly taken from us..." intoned the tall, white-haired minister, keeping his eyes trained on the pages in his Bible to hold his emotions in check. Claire had been an active, much loved member of the Congregational church; someone he could always count on to offer a kindness or do the right thing. He had worked late into the night to craft his eulogy, determined to do her memory justice, knowing his words would be but marginal comfort to the grief stricken family.

~

Claire Winslow had, indeed, been a pillar of the community, widely known and respected for her many charitable deeds. To accommodate the many people, strangers to Peter Winslow and his children, who wished to make their condolences known, it was deemed essential to host a public reception in the Meeting House next to the cemetery, immediately following the interment. It was necessary. For her many good deeds, she deserved to be widely mourned. Peter held his head high and stood with his children, accepting what seemed, at times, an endless succession of strangers, eager to offer their condolences.

Later, at the Winslow's beautiful shingle style seaside home, family members, close friends, and invited mourners flocked to pay their respects and do their best to celebrate the bountiful life that had been so tragically cut short. Cars, trucks, SUVs, and limousines lined the long driveway, and many other vehicles were pulled up along the edge of the expansive lawn at the height of the memorial gathering. As the evening approached, mourners started leaving the home in small groups, talking in quiet, emotionally drained tones as they made their way toward their respective cars.

Inside, a very somber Peter Winslow dutifully stood by the door, saying his good byes, accepting, as best he could, the many gestures of comfort. While a few mourners lingered, milling about or sitting on sofas or chairs, their voices were hushed. The beautiful furnishings, accented by massive and richly colored floral arrangements, had been a great source of pride and comfort, assembled with loving care by the departed hostess.

On an antique sideboard, an array of framed photographs, of various sizes, had been carefully arranged, obviously spanning each decade of Claire Winslow's life. Some photos were in color, some black and white, but all featured the beautiful daughter, wife, and mother, at different points in time in her life, alone and with various family members and friends. There were several stunningly beautiful professional photos from an earlier time when Claire had briefly been a model, but most of the pictures were decidedly of the "home photographer" variety, showing Claire with her two children, ranging in age from infant to adult.

Her father, Randolph, sat sadly in his wheelchair at one end of the sideboard, alone and in silence. His hands were clasped in his lap, and he gazed sadly at the photo display, tears steadily rolling down his cheeks, his head shaking ever so slightly. His burly attendant sat at a nearby table, eating his dinner, while keeping a watchful eye on his elderly charge. Yes, it was tough to lose a child. He felt compassion for Mr. Winthrop. But, this was a job, not a deep emotional attachment, so he ate with gusto from a heaping plate of food, enjoying one of the many perks of his fortunate employment.

At the same time, David and Anne were standing at the other end of the sideboard, talking wearily. David picked up a photo for closer examination, and Anne absently rubbed his back in a slow, comforting manner. David's eyes welled up as he looked at his mother, several years back, standing on the deck of a sailboat, her eyes smiling at the camera, her beautiful dark hair flying in the wind, and her arms lovingly wrapped around a young David and younger Amie. They had been sailing on Long Island Sound, he recalled, on one of many such wonderful family adventures.

Anne stopped rubbing David's back and stepped slightly to the right to pick up an old, black and white photo showing a handsome family of four. She turned it over and saw the neat inscription "Christmas, 1959" on the other side. Turning it back over, she carefully studied the photo of a stunningly beautiful, petite Isabella Winthrop, her dark hair pulled back in an elegant French twist, smiling happily as she stood next to a tall, distinguished looking Randoplh. A poised twelve year old Claire, nearly as tall as her mother and boasting strikingly similar features, her long dark hair flowing, was standing next to a tall, handsome sixteen year old Randolph "Randy" Winthrop, Jr., both smiling broadly.

"They look so happy..." Anne murmured.

"I know..." David replied wistfully, a furrow creasing his brow.

Anne sighed and carefully placed the photo back on the sideboard. She paused to look over at and contemplate Randolph for a brief moment, sitting sadly in his wheelchair. "I just realized that we don't seem to have any pictures here of you and Amie with your mother and grandfather," she said, looking back over the array of photos.

David glanced at Randolph, then shook his head and shrugged his shoulders slightly. "I don't know... I think we just spent a lot more time with Dad's family." He thought for a moment, quickly flipping through the years in his mind. "I don't think my mother was especially fond of Grandfather's wife," he concluded. "We never really talked about it, though."

Anne nodded her head slightly as she moved slowly along the sideboard, then stopped and pointed to a small black and white photo of a younger Claire holding a baby, a young boy sitting on a chair in front of her. "How old were you in this one?"

"Which one?" David asked, bending forward to look. "Oh... That one... I don't really know; Amie is obviously a baby, so I must be five or six..."

"Hmmm... You look a little older; Where was it taken?"

"I really don't know... I found it in Mom's dresser. Her face looks *so* beautiful – don't you think?"

"Absolutely..."

"I can't believe she's gone..."

"I know..."

"I keep thinking it had to be someone else in that wreck..." David confessed sadly. "It would make so much more sense!" Anne nodded silently and put a comforting arm around him. "I… I know this sounds a little crazy…" he continued, "but I find myself looking around — *seriously* — like I'm going to see her if I just look *hard* enough…"

~

Oblivious to David and Anne, two women were standing nearby, their backs to the array of framed photographs, heads close together, talking in confidential tones. "Oh… the poor man!" said the taller woman, the timbre of her voice stating quite clearly that she was looking at the handsome widower, calculating her prospects. "It's one thing to lose your wife in a horrible crash, but then to have her scandalous affair displayed in such a public way, *well*…"

"Do you think he had any idea, Betsy?" whispered the shorter woman, inclining her head toward her friend.

"Well! It was *so* obvious! I can't believe he had *no* idea!" She paused and looked over at Peter. "Though, I suppose, people sometimes only see what they want to see…"

"When did *you* know about it?"

"Why, the very first time I saw them together I knew!" the tall woman said, arching her eyebrows as if to make a point. "He was *gorgeous*, but it was shameful, how she looked at that young man! All gooey-eyed…" She inclined her head a bit, lowering the volume of her exchange. "She was *clearly* suffering from a *classic* case of empty-nest syndrome…" she concluded, her voice ripe with condescension. "I mean, with both her children off at school, and Peter traveling all the time…

Well! She was such a compulsive do-gooder, I suppose she thought nobody would notice!"

"You know what I don't understand? *Why* were they driving out on Beach Road?" queried the shorter woman, eager to add something to the scandalous talk.

"*Exactly*!" the taller woman exclaimed, raising her head in concert with her verbal punctuation. "And what was she *thinking*, letting *him* drive her Jag like they were in the Grand Prix?" She lowered her head again, along with her tone. "You know, I heard they *might* have had dinner in Newport and they *probably* had a drink or two… Between you and me, I *heard* he might have had a little problem with alcohol… Talk about flirting with danger!"

David, who had been quietly listening to this exchange over his shoulder for several minutes, determined that his tolerance had been exceeded at this point. He turned sharply toward the women, circling quickly around to face them, a frosty look on his face. "Ladies? I hope you'll excuse us, but it's been a long day…"

~

A half hour later, after the lingering guests had been dispatched and Randolph's muscular attendant had bundled him into his car to whisk him back to Boston, the Winslow family gathered in the living room to decompress. David and Anne sat together on the elegant brocade sofa, while an exhausted Amie sat opposite them on one of her mother's favorite pieces of furniture, a matching loveseat.

Peter, too exhausted to sit, was standing by a beautiful wingback chair, his hand resting firmly on the back for support. He was about to say something, when the doorbell suddenly chimed. He shook his head wearily and walked off to answer the door.

"Who in the world could that be?" Amie asked with a hint of petulance.

"Probably those vultures circling back to see if there is anything else they can pick up to gossip about," responded Anne without skipping a beat.

David frowned. "It's O.K., really... Let them talk..."

"No it isn't O.K.!" Anne was quick to rejoin.

"I agree with Anne," Amie added bitterly. "Those old cows should have stayed home if they didn't know how to keep their mouths shut."

"Look..." David countered, "I am *not* defending them... They *shouldn't* be saying these things, *here* – of *all* places! But let's be realistic! The truth is, you can't stop people from... *speculating*..." Raising his hands momentarily in a gesture of exasperation, he continued. "It's not like it was all completely baseless! Let's be honest: *All* this *talk*... it's because the circumstances are so... *suspicious*... and there are so *many* unanswered questions! People just want to understand... Hell! *I* want to understand! You know... How *could* this have ever happened? I mean... the *way* she died..."

He paused as Amie wiped away tears and Anne sat, eyes downcast. "I... I just don't understand..." he continued. "What *was* she doing with him at the beach in the first place? Why was she letting *him* drive her car?"

At that moment, Peter came back into the room, looking strained and exhausted. Amie immediately turned her focus on him and asked, "Who was it, Dad?" happy to change the subject.

Peter sighed. "Chief Macomber..." he responded. "He wanted to drop by to offer his official condolences and update me on the investigation..." He paused as all eyes looked at him in expectation. "He just returned some of your mother's things..." he explained, his voice cracking slightly. He cleared his throat quickly and went on to say, "Doug is still in a coma, so there really isn't anything new to report."

David closed his eyes for a second and took a deep breath. Looks were exchanged around the room, but no one knew what to say anymore.

"I'm exhausted," Peter concluded finally. "I think we should all try to get some rest," he added, turning sadly toward the hallway that would lead to his lonely Master Suite.

Three

I t was pitch black beyond the windows, as far as the eye could see. The interior of the vintage silver Jaguar was a deep red leather, beautifully and lovingly maintained in pristine condition. It was one of Claire's most treasured possessions, a 1960 prototype XK-E; a gift to her mother, Isabella, from her father, Randolph, presented with great fanfare to mark her mother's thirty-sixth birthday. Stored under cover in the car barn for two decades, her father had delivered it to her without ceremony, as if he were passing a baton in a relay exercise. It did not matter. Claire had been moved to tears then, and had treated this gift with the greatest love and respect throughout her many years of stewardship.

Now, however, something wasn't right. Claire sat in the passenger seat, a confused look of terror etched on her face. She glanced out into the blackness, then turned her head, fixing her gaze on the unseen driver, a frantic look of pleading in her eyes, imploring him to slow down.

Suddenly she let out a blood curdling scream, throwing up her hands in a futile protective gesture as the car crashed and folded into her…

Four

"**M**om!!!"

David sat bolt upright as he screamed out for his mother. Slowly coming to the realization that he was safe, in his bed, at home in Westport, he dropped his head forward, cupping it in his hands, pushing in on his temples as if trying to squash the dream out of his consciousness.

Anne, awakened from a deep sleep by the noise, rolled toward him. "David?... Honey?..." she asked in a gentle voice still full of sleep. "It's O.K.... You must have had that dream again..."

"I'm sorry..." David replied, his head still in his hands.

"It's O.K.... It was just that dream..."

"She must have been so scared..."

"I know, Sweetie..."

"It had to be *so* horrible..."

"I know..."

"I'm sorry..."

"It's O.K.... Just close your eyes, honey, and think about something else..."

"It's not that easy…" David said, lifting his head, looking straight ahead, afraid that looking at Anne might release the tears welling up behind his eyes.

"I know… But try… You need to get some sleep…" Anne said gently, rubbing his back with concern.

David sat quietly for a minute then threw back the bed covers and stood up. "I'm going to go get some water…" he said, reaching for his robe. "Maybe a little something to eat…"

"Do you want me to come?" Anne asked, propping herself up on an elbow.

"No… You go back to sleep… I'll be O.K.…."

"You're so exhausted…"

"I won't be long…"

~

Standing at the kitchen island, David slowly picked at some of the food which he had pulled out of the refrigerator. In spite of the fact that they had had so many visitors after the funeral, there was still an abundance of food left over. "Mother would have planned this better…" he thought sadly, rewrapping a casserole dish and putting it away.

He pulled out a milk carton and poured a glass of milk. "Mother would have had bottled milk…" he thought, looking at the disposable carton sitting on the counter. She had always gone out of her way to get milk and other liquids in glass containers. The taste was better, she had maintained — and she was right, as usual.

David rubbed his forehead then turned and look in the cabinet next to the refrigerator. Shuffling a few things around, he finally located a bottle of Excedrin, plucked it out and closed the cabinet door. David wrestled opened the cover as he returned to the island, shook a couple of tablets out into his hand, and popped them into his mouth, chasing them down with a long swallow of milk.

Carefully, he picked up after himself, putting things away as his mother had always done. Looking around the kitchen, he sadly realized that she would never walk into this room again, yet she was everywhere. Nothing in the house didn't remind him of his mother. This was her domain.

Turning off the lights, David wandered out of the kitchen, toward the front hallway. As if by habit, he checked the front door and reached to turn off a light that had been left on. Glancing at the entry table, he noticed an odd plastic bag, looking strangely out of place. Curiosity getting the best of him, he opened it and looked inside, freezing in his tracks, an agonized look sweeping into his eyes. He closed the bag quickly and set it down, backing away a step or two. He stood there, his eyes fixated on the bag, as if paralyzed.

"Chief Macomber must have brought it..." he finally reasoned, thinking back to the last caller of the day. He had quickly realized that the bag contained his mother's purse and other small personal items that had been salvaged from the crash. After a bought of inertia that seemed eternal, David carefully picked up the bag again and turned off the hall light.

Moving slowly into the living room, carrying the bag gingerly, as if it contained a poisonous substance,

David lit the brass lamp on the side table and wearily sat down on the sofa, depositing the bag on the coffee table.

He sat there, looking at the plastic bag, but when he closed his eyes he could see his mother smiling — laughing, really – showing off her new little puppy, nestled safely in that very shoulder bag. He opened his eyes as tears hung on the tips of his lashes, slowly reaching out to take the plastic bag back in hand, gathering it into his lap.

Gently, he emptied the contents onto the coffee table. With careful deliberation, he started sifting through the items, touching each in turn with a tender, almost reverential manner. It was possible, he thought, knowing it was crazy, that he might connect with some lingering essence of his mother, considering the fact that these things were with her in her final moments.

He sat up straight when he saw the set of keys, his focus zeroing in on the car key. Had this been the one? Contemplating it for a long moment, he concluded that his mother had probably handed over the spare set, not the one in front of him with her house keys on the ring. Picking them up, he leaned back on the sofa, pressing the keys to his heart, his eyes closed lightly, shutting off his tears.

~

Claire was sitting in the passenger seat of her silver Jaguar, a beautiful smile on her face, looking at the unseen driver, her hand outstretched with the keys...

~

David shook his head as he quickly opened his eyes. He couldn't go there again. Not now... He couldn't watch her die again.

He was about to put the keys down when an odd shape caught his attention. Looking closely, a puzzled expression on his face, David realized that it was a Post Office box key on her ring. Odd. He couldn't remember any mention by his parents about having a Post office box.

Carefully, David put his mother's belongings back in the plastic bag, but put the keys in his bathrobe pocket before turning off the light and heading back to bed.

Five

November 26, 2006

The sun rose the next morning, as if there was nothing at all amiss with the world, bursting forth from the edge of the ocean in vivid shades of orange, pink, and yellow, reflected as whimsical wisps of brilliance along the bottom edges of the puffy clouds that decorated the sky.

The Morning Room had been Claire's favorite. Getting up before dawn, she was known to sit quietly in the dark, a fresh mug of coffee in hand, watching in awe through the massive windows as the beauty of the sunrise was unveiled over Buzzards Bay. "Every day is different," she had maintained, as far back as David could remember. "Every morning is special!"

It had been their "special time", particularly in those years when he was the only one. He had been conditioned, by osmosis as much as anything, he thought, to wake up at five each morning, like clockwork, ensuring a personalized start to every day. Dad would be in the shower or already off somewhere for his work, but Mother had always been there for him, with very few exceptions. Seven wonderful years when the sun rose and set for him alone, until Amie came along and changed the rhythm of their lives.

He really hadn't had much use for that cranky little baby, especially during his morning ritual with his mother. He tolerated her because he had to, but he was not among those who had welcomed her into their lives. Amie hadn't gotten his stamp of approval, in fact, until she was old enough to take up skiing. She had proved from the very start to be fearless on the slopes, and was naturally very talented. David's grudging acknowledgement of her talent had slowly given way to true admiration. She was six and he was thirteen.

They had been the first skiers on the slopes on many mornings, with and without their parents, often in concert with the first colorful rays of dawn, and David soon discovered that their age difference was magically evened out when they jumped off the ski lift and set out to conquer the mountain together.

On this day, however, David sat there alone, conjuring up his last morning with his mother. It had been late August. They had shared a brilliant crimson sunrise, with bold strokes of red splashed across the horizon, amid much speculation about the sailors' plight.

"Red sun in morning, sailors take warning..." she had chided him with a gentle poke. "You can forget that trip to Cuttyhunk, young man..."

Now, the sun hung in the sky like a bright yellow ball, transforming the ocean into a panoramic stretch of sparkling fluid motion before his eyes, as David gazed sadly out the windows to the East. Long beams of sunlight stretched across the room, highlighting the brilliance of the fresh floral arrangements that adorned the sideboard and table. David looked around the room, quietly noting how the light so dramatically enhanced the already beautiful setting, all in stark contrast to the prevailing mood of the home.

Before long, Alice arrived and set about her sacred new

task of organizing a healthy breakfast for the grieving family. Alice had for many years been Claire's right hand when it came to major Spring and Fall cleanings, party preparations, and dinner gatherings. She had been the logical one to turn to. Who else would know exactly what Claire would have done to keep her family together and well cared for? Peter had been greatly relieved when she readily accepted his proposal to extend and expand her employment.

Soon, the smell of bacon, eggs, and warm muffins filled the air, inviting the obviously sleep deprived household to the table.   The table floral arrangement had been carefully centered at Claire's usual place at the West end of the oblong table, circumventing the need for anyone to have to think about occupying her chair so soon after her passing. "Her Windsor chairs..." Alice had thought. "So perfect for this room..." More than once, Alice knew for certain, Claire had admired their gently arching frames, noting how the spindled backs suggested the rising sun. In time, Alice thought she would rearrange the room a bit to make it easier for Peter and the children, perhaps removing the table leaf to make the table round, and moving Claire's chair over next to the sideboard. Yes, a simple way to change the look; she would sort it out in time.

"You ready for breakfast, Sweetie?" she asked kindly, acknowledging Jack, Claire's sad little Cairn Terrier, knowing he could not understand where his Mommy had gone – or that she wouldn't be coming back...

~

"I'm so sorry I can't stay longer, Dad," Amie said softly as everyone sat quietly around the table, each one picking at their breakfast. "but I *have* to get back to Paris. The timing just couldn't be any worse..."

"I know..." Peter responded gently, reaching out to squeeze his daughter's hand. "It's O.K...."

"I promise I'll be back as soon as the internship is over..." Amie continued, clearly conflicted by her decision to keep her previously planned travel arrangements in play. It was supposed to have been a brief Thanksgiving break, not a tragic, life altering gathering. "I'm sorry, but I've worked so hard..."

"I know! It's O.K., Princess. Mother was *so* proud of you, and she would be the first one to say you should carry on! She..." Peter paused, casting his gaze down for a moment and taking a deep breath. "Your mother really loved Paris..." he continued, looking directly at Amie, his sad eyes glistening. "She would be *very* upset with you, young lady, if you let this... if you didn't get right back and press on with your career. Your Mother was *so* excited for you..."

"Dad's right..." David jumped in as his father blinked back tears. "This meant a lot to Mom! She actually told me that she was making room in her closet for all those designer clothes you were *destined* to create for her!" he said, reaching for a lighter moment from the past. "She even joked that she was planning to make a comeback in her modeling career..." He paused and forced a smile. "Mother would be completely pissed if you messed up this great opportunity because of... her..."

"I know!" Amie cried softly.

"We'll be here as much as possible..." Anne said, gently touching Amie's arm in a comforting gesture.

Peter threw back his shoulders and cleared his throat.

A . G a r d n e r   S t r o n g

"I don't need anyone hanging around here, worrying about me. Jack and I will be fine…"

"Look at the time!" Anne gasped, suddenly taking note of her watch. "We should get going! Security lines at Logan are going to be brutal!"

"I don't want to think about it…" Amie groaned, wiping her tears as she pushed back her chair so she could stand. "Do you want to come along for the ride, Dad?"

"Thanks! No… I have to take care of some paperwork; legal stuff…"

David exchanged a quick look of concern with Amie and Anne. "Anne… Can you take Amie to Boston O.K.?"

"Sure…" Anne responded, surprised but ever supportive, nodding her head slightly. "Can we use your car?"

"You don't need to stay here, David. Go ahead with Anne and your sister. I'll be fine!" Peter said as he took a sip of coffee.

"I'm a little tired…" David demurred, "I'd prefer to stay with you, Dad – No offense, ladies! Here…"

David stood up and reached into his pocket, pulling out two sets of keys. He handed one set to Anne and gave her a hug. Looking at the other keys for a moment, he put them back in his pocket and turned to Amie. "Have a safe trip…" he cautioned, giving her a hug.

Amie moved to the head of the table and gave her father a big hug and kiss, then turned to Anne, her eyes filed with tears. "See you later!" she exclaimed, forcing a smile. Anne gave David a brief look, then herded Amie out of the room.

"More coffee, Dad?" David offered, picking up the pot.

"Yes... Thanks..." Peter replied with a nod, extending his cup toward his son.

David poured the coffee for his father, then topped off his own cup before sitting down. "Dad..." he queried, a puzzled look settling on his face. "Why did you and Mom get a Post Office box?"

"What? We don't have a Post Office box! The mail is delivered here, to the house... You know that!"

"Well, that's what I thought. So..." David scratched his head, almost involuntarily. "Why does Mom have a Post Office key?"

"What?" Peter asked, looking genuinely puzzled. "I don't have any idea what you're talking about, David. Where did you get the idea that your mother has a Post Office key? Who told you this?"

David pulled the keys from his pocket and put them on the table. "Nobody said anything, Dad; I found it..." David paused as he separated the keys so the mail box key was easy to see. "It was with Mother's things — in that bag in the hallway; I found it last night." He looked at his father then back at the key. "I had a really hard time sleeping last night and happened to wander into the front hallway... I guess you must have just left the bag there..."

Peter looked at the keys, visibly shaken. "Yes… I see… Well… I have no idea, David. It most likely has something to do with the church group, or one of the charities she works… worked on."

David pulled the keys back and considered this. "I didn't think of that…"

Peter cleared his throat. "Well… it's nothing, son. I'm sure Harry – you know who I mean: that nice clerk at the Post Office – he can tell us who to return it to." He paused, then reached out to touch David's hand, ready to change the subject. "When did you say you have to go back to New Haven?"

David shrugged his shoulders. "I don't have to rush right back, Dad." He paused, looking out the window for a moment before looking back at his father. "In fact, I was actually thinking about skipping the next semester."

"Why would you want to do that?" Peter asked, sitting straight up, a new look of concern on his face.

"I don't think I can really focus just yet…"

Peter blinked, his mind whirling, uncomfortable with the sudden realization that he was now a single parent. "Your mother wouldn't approve…"

"It isn't the same as Amie…" David protested, anticipating his father's words.

"How do you figure that?" Peter asked, in a stern yet gentle fatherly tone, leaning in toward his son.

David looked out the window for a moment then turned to look at his father. "Amie has a unique opportunity to advance her career. The fashion industry is pretty cut-throat, as far as I can see anyway. She can't slack off – for any reason. My situation is totally different: I'm just in grad school. It isn't uncommon at all for students take a break to travel or…"

"You want to travel?" Peter pressed, taking a sip of his coffee.

"No… No… I just…"

Peter put down his coffee cup and leaned back in his chair. "Well, you don't need to stick around here and worry about me, David…"

"It's not that, Dad…"

"What is it then?"

David put a strawberry in his mouth and chewed slowly for a moment before responding. "I have too much on my mind, I guess… I mean, I just can't stop thinking about… *everything*…" He paused and took a sip of his coffee. "I'm really not sleeping much… and when I do, I just have these awful, vivid dreams, over and over… You know… about Mother… about the accident…"

"You just have to pull yourself together," Peter said kindly, but with studied firmness. "Stop thinking about it." He looked sadly at David's troubled face, knowing he was advising himself as well as his son. "I'm going to get back to work, and you should do the same."

"It's not that easy…"

Peter took a deep breath. "We just have to force our-
selves to focus on… *other* things…" He looked down
at his breakfast plate, then back at his son. "I was thinking I might try and spend more time in New York for
awhile…" He paused, looking around sadly. "It
would be strange, coming home to… Well, you
know… It was just the two of us, with you and Amie
off to school…" Peter paused then cleared his throat.
"Alice can help me with Jack… But your mother
expects — expected – great things for you too, David.
You need to get back to school and sink your teeth back
into your studies."

"But she would want me to do my best, Dad," David
responded quickly, "and I'm not sure I *can* just yet…"

"What does Anne think?"

"Anne? I don't know, Dad; We haven't talked about
it…" David looked out the window. "There's just been
so much going on…" he turned back to his father, "and,
to be honest, I really just thought about it seriously this
morning, when she was still sleeping."

Peter settled back in his chair, concern etched clearly on
his face. Reflexively, he rubbed his forehead. "Well,
let's say you took off some time – Let's say you skipped
this next semester… What would you do instead? Get
a job? Work for awhile? Do you want me to get you an
internship with my firm?"

"I don't know…"

Peter bowed his head and rubbed his forehead as if trying to clear his head. "What's really troubling you,

David?" he said looking back at David, "...Above and beyond the obvious?"

"Oh... I don't know, Dad... Like I said: I'm just not sleeping... I try, but I close my eyes I can't stop imagining Mom... What it was like... How scared she must have been... And I'm so confused about why she was letting that guy drive her car... I mean... He was the damn carpenter, for God's sake! She never even let *me* drive that car!"

"Well, she bought you your own classic MGB, David. I don't see how you can complain about not driving her car..."

"That's not the point, Dad! Why did she let *him* drive the Jag?"

"Well, I'm sure she was just trying to be kind..." Peter offered softly.

"Kind?!!!" David exploded. "Kind is a hot meal, Dad, not handing the keys to your vintage Jaguar to someone who is going to drive like a maniac and kill you!"

"David..."

"I'm sorry, Dad..."

"You don't have to apologize..."

"I'm sorry... I really am, but I go over and over it and it makes no sense..."

"You know your mother always went above and beyond helping everyone..."

"I know... I know..."

Peter signed, then leaned back in toward David. "Doug is the son of those people in Maine that your mother helps so much."

"I know; you said that before... But, I don't really know who they are."

"People who worked for her parents."

"Do you know them?"

Peter thought for a moment. "Well... No, not really. I knew your mother was involved with them from the past, but I never went up there or had anything to do with them. We always summered on Block Island – well, you know that!"

"Why was Mom so involved with them?"

"Your mother felt an obligation..." Peter paused, his brow knit as he thought. "...because of her mother, I think. She spent Summers up on that island as a child... And that was where her mother died; I think she's actually buried up there."

"What did Mom do for these people?"

Peter arched his eyebrows. "Financial support mostly... She helped Doug with work; and I think there was a time when they were afraid they might lose their house – you know... property taxes or something – and your mother helped them out... Used her mother's money..."

"Have you talked to them?"

"Doug's parents? No... I probably should. I'm not sure if they even came down to the hospital. They are quite elderly, I believe..."

"*They* haven't reached out to you, Dad?"

"Well... Doug is in a coma, son. They have enough on their plate..."

"But, he *killed* Mom..."

"It was an accident, David..."

"Ninety miles an hour on that winding road was no accident!"

"Your mother probably encouraged him..."

"No way! No way, Dad! Did you ever drive with her?"

"Of course I drove with her..."

"Mother was a nut about speed limits! You know that, Dad! And she loved that car!"

Peter sat a little taller, his frustration evident. "What are you trying to say?"

"Nothing, Dad... I'm sorry..."

Six

November 27, 2006

There is a charming Post Office building at Westport Point, offering a quaint atmosphere and convenient location from which to serve the Southernmost inhabitants of Westport, but the main Post Office, with the best hours of operation, opening daily at 5:30 a.m. and staying open until 3:00 p.m. on Saturdays, is a simple, boxy brick structure located on the state highway at the North end of town. While many held their boxes at the Point like a symbol of prestige, a good number of postal patrons had come to this office specifically, driving miles out of their way at times, drawn by convenient hours and the helpfulness and sunny disposition of the mild mannered Harry, everyone's favorite postal clerk.

David stood patiently in line, clutching his mother's keys in his hand, his mind wandering. It was easy to slip into a state of suspended reality, standing there, among strangers. David tried to imagine his mother doing the same, but the picture was fuzzy.

The person at the counter finally finished their business and stepped aside, making room for David to move up to the desk. He laid his mother's keys on the counter, pointing to the Post Office key.

Harry smiled brightly as he looked directly at David and asked "How can I help you?"

"I was wondering if you could identify this key for me?" David asked tentatively.

"Excuse me?" Harry responded, a puzzled look on his face.

David cleared his throat and softly offered, "My mother, Claire Winslow..."

"Oh, *yes!*" Harry quickly caught on. "Mrs. Winslow... She was always so nice..." he said, shaking his head sympathetically. "Such a tragedy..."

"Thank you," David said, feeling more than a little uncomfortable. "Can you identify this key for me so I can return it?"

"You want to close the box?" Harry asked, furrowing his brow as he pushed his glasses back up his nose.

"No, I just need to know who I can return the key to."

"Well, I can take the key here," Harry said, rubbing his forehead just above his right eye, "but I think you might need to do some paperwork to close the box." He stepped back one step. "I think she has some mail, though; Just a minute..." Harry turned and walked softly off through a door to the right of the desk. David watched, a mild frustration gathering, like storm clouds, on his face.

Harry returns a moment later with two envelopes in his hand. "Here you go..."

David's tension eased as he reached out to take the envelopes, his frustration turning into a blend of curiosity and trepidation. He examined the envelopes quickly, a puzzled look on his face. One was from an attorney in Portland, Maine, the other from someone on North Island, Maine, both addressed to his mother. "What is the name on the box?" he asked.

Harry, deliberately oblivious to the line growing behind David, spilling quickly into the outer lobby, patiently pulled out a ledger and started flipping through the pages. "Your mother… let me see… yes, just 'Claire Winslow'…"

"Really? Just my mother? Are you sure?"

Harry pushed up his glasses again and looked back at the ledger. "Yes, well… She recently renewed her box rental, so she's paid up through the end of next October." He paused and looked at David with compassion in his eyes. "Under the circumstances, I think you either have to close the box or switch it to another name, but I think you need to do some paperwork either way. Just a minute…" Harry turned and walked off through another door to the back, leaving David to stare at the two envelopes in his hand.

Seven

Westport, a natural haven nestled securely between Dartmouth, Massachusetts, and the eastern edge of Rhode Island, about an hour's drive South of Boston, is known for it's dairy products, wine, Macomber squash, acres of thick forest, and miles of sandy beach. The Westport coastline is a favorite for beach and boating enthusiasts who don't want to tangle with the traffic on the Cape.

Bordered to the North-West by South Watuppa Pond and Sawdy Pond, and, boasting over eight miles of direct frontage on Buzzards Bay and approximately thirty-five miles of shoreline between the East and West Branch of the Westport River and its estuary, Westport was known historically for its whaling industry and rum-running enterprises.

Settled in 1670 and incorporated in 1787, Westport has a heritage rich in American history. Being the western-most portion of the coastal tract that was purchased from the Wampanoag Indians in 1652 by the elders of the Plymouth Colony, stretching from what is now the Town of Fairhaven, the land was subsequently sold in smaller parcels to Quakers and Baptists who were hoping to escape religious persecution. Westport Point had originally been used by the Indians as a summer encampment, called "Pacquachuck" or "cleared hill", where they engaged in farming and fishing.

Horseneck Beach has been maintained as a State Reservation by the Commonwealth of Massachusetts and the Department of Environmental Management since 1956.

The westernmost portion of the central peninsula is known as Cherry & Webb Beach, and is managed by the Town. Between the two stretches of land, tourists and residents are offered magnificent stretches of sandy white beaches and the whimsical drifts of the dunes.

Agriculture and fishing remain vital components of Westport's economy, but tourism has grown dramatically since the 1960's when Interstate 195 and Route 88 were constructed to provide easy access to Horseneck Beach. Although Westport has become more of a bedroom community, in recent years, for people working in Boston and Providence, its population of nearly fourteen thousand has had little impact on the rural flavor of its sixty-one square miles.

Because it was late November, there were no crowds of sunbathers gathered at the beach this day, and David was able to walk up the sandy path from the Cherry and Webb parking lot and find a solitary spot at the high point, on the top of the dune to the right of the path. He sat there quietly, leaning forward slightly, his arms folded on his bent knees, his left hand clutching two unopened envelopes. His eyes were fixed on a point well beyond the clean gray sands of the beach. To a casual observer passing by along the path, he seemed to be watching the tidal shift of Buzzards Bay, but, in truth, his gaze never encompassed the rising waters or the impact on the beach as the waves rolled in and receded, rhythmic and unrelenting.

David remained this way, as if transfixed, occasionally tapping the envelopes in his hands, but never looking at them. Eventually, after what seemed like an hour, but was, in truth, more like fifteen minutes, he shifted his eyes and considered the envelopes carefully.

He would not take this to his father. Not yet, anyway.

If his mother had been having an affair, had she taken it to the point of consulting a lawyer? It was hard enough for David to contemplate the implications; he couldn't take the chance of causing further devastation to his father.

David took a deep breath, and, hesitating only for an additional fraction of a moment, opened the letter from Attorney James Strong in Portland, Maine.

It was typed, neatly and in perfect form, on the letter-head of a Portland law firm by the name of Drum-mondWoodsum. It was dated November 21, 2006, and was brief and to the point:

"Dear Mrs. Winslow,
I have prepared the deeds and will, as you requested. Please contact my office at your earliest convenience so we can discuss how you wish to proceed. I will be out of the office until November 28, 2006, but will be available to assist you anytime after that.

Best wishes for a good Thanksgiving with your extended family.

Sincerely,

James A. Strong, Esq."

So official; So neat; So precise; So entirely and incomprehensibly at odds with the known facts, to say nothing of the uncertainty and turmoil in David's mind. Almost involuntarily, he carefully scrutinized the envelope, as if some new, clarifying information might be revealed. No mention of separation or divorce, that was good. But a will and deeds? What was that about? Dad had mentioned meeting with their friend from

Newport, Attorney Lowenstein, to deal with Mother's will and other legal maters. What did it mean that she had apparently gone, secretly and on her own, to some other lawyer, in Maine no less, to draft a new will? He shifted back to the letter and pondered the neatly typed words for a few minutes more as if that would somehow alter the words or add some new clarity to the message. Shaking his head, he quickly refolded the page and returned it to it's original sheathing, taking in a deep breath before he stuffed the envelope into his pocket.

David looked up at a pair of seagulls, hovering nearby in the strong sea breeze, like invisibly anchored but unattended winged kites. He sat like that for several minutes, then focused slowly, almost reluctantly, on the second, handwritten envelope. After a long moment's hesitation, he opened the envelope with the return address of:

> Mrs. Samuel Brown
> 163 Island Road
> North Island, Maine

Inside, David found a one page handwritten note, on light blue note paper, dated November 22, 2006. The handwriting was somewhat irregular and a little difficult to read, appearing to have been written by someone with an arthritic hand:

> "Dearest Claire,
> I realize you won't get this now until
> after Thanksgiving, but I just wanted to
> let you know that we are ever thankful

for all that you have done. Your kindness far outweighs ours.

I hope Douglas is happy and feeling more
at home.

God bless you always!
Love, Elsie"

He read the note again, blinking furiously to hold back any sign of emotion, then refolded it with studied deliberation and carefully slipped it back into the now slightly wrinkled envelope.

He lifted his gaze and fixed it, once again, on the powerfully modulating swells of Buzzards Bay and, almost peripherally, the waves crashing onto the beach. His face was a mask of turbulent detachment; His focus, in truth, was about two hundred miles or so across the water.

Eight

November 28, 2006

The sun was barely peeking up over the horizon when David tossed a small travel bag on the back seat of his car. Anne huddled next to him in a long wool coat, her hair still tangled by sleep and her face a mask of concern.

David turned to Anne and put his arms around her. "I won't be gone more than two days, I promise…" he said giving her a quick kiss. "Maybe a day if I make all the right connections…"

"I don't understand why you can't just call…" Anne complained.

"I just think that I have to see their faces…" David responded, turning to get in the car.

"So, why can't I come?" Anne persisted.

"We can't leave Dad alone…" David asserted with a hint of frustration, shaking his head as he shut the car door. He quickly turned on the ignition so he could put down the window. "Not just yet…" he continued, his tone mollifying.

Anne was not appeased. "Why can't you wait?"

David pulled the folded MapQuest directions out of his pocket and tucked it above the visor for easy reference. "No," he said as he turned back toward Anne, a serious look on his face. "I need to see this new will…"

"But, it obviously wasn't signed, so it's meaningless..." she persisted, "Don't you see?"

"I know that..." David said with a hint of impatience, "but it might give me a clue; The deeds too..."

Anne was not satisfied. "I still don't see why you can't wait..."

David reached his arms out the window and pulled Anne toward him, giving her another kiss. "I won't be gone long... I promise..."

David forced a smile, then closed his window and drove off down the long driveway. Anne... He knew she meant well... She just didn't understand. He focused on the roadway ahead and never looked back, even knowing that Anne was probably still standing there, watching him disappear.

~

Three and a half hours later, David pulled into the parking lot along the working waterfront in Portland, Maine. He got out of the car, looked at the lawyer's envelope, then let his eyes scan up and down the street until he saw what he was looking for. He glanced back at the waterfront and tried to imagine his mother coming to this foreign place. Had she driven up here to secretly meet with this lawyer, or had she taken the train from Boston? Both were entirely possible, of course. A day trip, either way.

He crossed the street and entered the brick building of DrummondWoodsum, looking for the office directory. He took the elevator to the fourth floor and walked over to the pleasant receptionist who seemed to sit at the center of activity. He consulted the envelope again before he asked, "Attorney James Strong?"

"Certainly! Do you have an appointment?" she asked brightly.

"No…" It hadn't occurred to him that he would need an appointment to see a Maine lawyer. He had never been to Maine, but his impression had been that it was a vast land populated by potato farmers and lobstermen. He reprimanded himself silently for his arrogant assumptions and made a quick mental note that he should take some time to explore parts of the country that he did not know first hand.

"I think he might be available," the receptionist said with a smile. "What is your name?"

"David Winslow," he replied hopefully.

"Will Attorney Strong know what this is in reference to?" she asked.

"My mother," he said softly, "Claire Winslow."

After a brief exchange, the receptionist had ushered David into a modest but comfortable conference room, where he sat waiting. Within about ten minutes, a tall, slender man, wearing an open collared shirt and a handsome sweater from L.L.Bean, entered the room and extended a hand. "Mr. Winslow," he said warmly, "I'm Attorney Strong."

"Hi" David said tentatively as the attorney sat down, directly opposite him.

"How can I help you?" Attorney Strong asked, still smiling.

David took out the attorney's letter addressed to his mother, a newspaper clipping about the accident, and the published obituary. He passed them to the attorney and sat quietly watching as Attorney Strong skimmed through the documents in front if him, his face growing more troubled with each passing moment.

"I am stunned by this news, Mr. Winslow…" Attorney Strong said in muted, somber tones as he sat back in his chair.

"David, please…"

"David…" the attorney continued, "I am so sorry… Claire – Mrs. Winslow – was such a lovely person…"

"Thank you…" David said, leaning forward. "I was hoping to get a copy of the will and deeds so we can sort out her… *affairs.*"

Attorney Strong looked uncomfortable. He shifted in his seat and cleared his throat before responding. "I understand your situation, David, but even with your mother's death, I'm just not at liberty to share my client files with you."

"Excuse me?" David responded, his surprise clearly evident. He had not expected any resistance. "Surely the attorney-client privilege does not survive when the client is dead!"

Attorney Strong leaned forward and shook his head. "That's not the case, actually. The attorney has a duty of loyalty as well as a duty to maintain inviolate the confidences of a former or present client, and these duties survive the death of the client," he explained. "I cannot share any information with any of my client's family without specific permission…"

"But, that's crazy!" David protested. "My mother was making a new will! Surely that's information she intended to share with us!" He persisted, incredulous "And what about the deeds? Our home is in Massachusetts. Why would she be having an attorney in *Maine* write deeds for her? For what property?" David asked, throwing his hands up in exasperation.

Attorney Strong leaned back in his chair and asked calmly, "Did you discuss this with your father? Perhaps he and your mother talked about…"

David shook his head. "I don't think so; He had no idea she even had a Post Office box. He… He was away a lot…" David began to look uncomfortable. He cleared his throat. "My Dad is devastated by this. He knows what people are saying and he can't accept that Mom was…" He leaned forward and swallowed hard. "…having an affair with this… carpenter…"

Attorney Strong looking stricken. "Affair? An affair with Douglas Brown? No… That's not possible!"

"Do you *know* him?"

"Douglas? No…" he shook his head. "No, not directly; But if your concern is about Claire's – your mother's – reputation…"

"That isn't it!" David interrupted. "I want to understand how this man was in a position to take the wheel of that car and kill my mother!"

"It had to be an accident..." Attorney Strong mussed, shaking his head. "A really *tragic* accident..."

"That's what my Dad says! 'It was an accident'..." David shook his head. "Doesn't *anyone* but me question what *right* this jerk had to be driving my mother's car at ninety miles an hour on a winding coastal road?"

"I can't answer that, but I'm *sure* it was an accident..."

"He was driving *ninety* miles an hour! Why? How does that just happen?" David demanded. "This... *stranger*... is *safe* in a hospital bed, but my mother is..."

"Did you talk with him?"

David slumped slightly, letting out a deep breath. "No; He's still in a coma..."

Attorney Strong shook his head, his expression one of great sympathy. "I'm sorry, I truly am," he said, "and I can't answer your questions for you, but I hope you can trust me and put your mind at ease on this one score: Your mother was *not* having an affair; I am positive about this."

"How can you be so certain?" David asked, his eyes moist with unshed tears.

"I can't elaborate," he said softly, shaking his head. "I am duty-bound to preserve your mother's confidences..." he continued gently, "but your mother was *not* having an affair with Douglas Brown."

Nine

The North Island ferry makes the twenty-five mile round trip to Rockland three times a day, weather permitting, excluding Thanksgiving and Christmas. In years past, the "weather permitting" caveat was only invoked when the Thoroughfare between North and South Islands was frozen over, making passage impossible, but since being sued for damage by an irate tourist (whose fancy sport car had been tossed sideways into a dump truck during a crossing through rough seas), the ferry service had been quick to curtail service every time the wind blew up from the South.

On this particular late November day, the ocean waters were relatively calm as the ferry left Rockland Harbor. It moved smoothly through the marked channel, past the fish processing plants and Coast Guard station, then steadily out of the sheltered waters, past the massive breakwater. Forty-five feet wide at the top, it had been crafted from more than seven-hundred thousand tons of locally quarried granite over a period of about twenty years in the late 1800s. Designed to protect the harbor and waterfront structures from the ferocious Nor'easters that periodically storm into the Mid-Coast area, the approximately eight-tenths of a mile long barrier had been permanently delineated since October 30, 1902, by the distinctive Rockland Breakwater Lighthouse, it's white beacon flashing almost forty feet above the water at high tide.

As the ferry slipped effortlessly into the open waters of Penobscot Bay, the distant profile of land mass guided the captain's hand and quietly fermented mixed expectations in David's thoughts.

~

David stood on the bow of the ferry as it entered the Thoroughfare and approached the dock. He shivered as he scanned the quaint, picturesque village of North Island, rising up in near story-book perfection from the water's edge. Though he had never been here before, the scene felt incredibly familiar, like a Currier and Ives that had been hanging in the upstairs hallway for as long as he could remember.

He pulled the two envelopes from his pocket and shuffled them so he could focus on the return address of the handwritten one. The ferry softly banged against the bumper pads that lined the dock, like silent black sentries, on guard against the occasionally less than smooth landing. The safety chains were hauled back to fully expose the bow end as the ramp was lowered and the crew prepared to unload.

The cars and trucks, directed by an energetic, no-nonsense female crew member, quickly rolled off the deck as David waited impatiently. When the last truck noisily crossed the threshold, David quickly followed on foot.

As he walked up the gangplank, he glanced briefly over at Brown's Boat Shop. This was surely the heartbeat of the little town, David surmised, noting the many boats stored in the yard.

He then fixed his attention on the people hovering near the top of the ramp, looking at him with great curiosity as he approached. He wondered if they were all waiting for someone, though it felt more like they were there just to watch the ferry load and unload, like the ticker at the bottom of the cable news shows, telegraphing the headlines of the day. David smiled weakly and let his eyes wander to the buildings framing the gateway to the tiny village.

As soon as David set foot on the dark pavement of the ferry landing parking lot, he started looking, without success, for signs of a taxi stand. It had not occurred to him that all the trappings of civilization might not be available to him when he got off the ferry. It was, after all, only twelve miles or so off the mainland!

"You look lost there young fella..." a rugged looking islander ventured, an amused smile dancing on his lips beneath a mountain of wild facial hair.

Startled by both his looks and his unsolicited offer of help, David looked at him hopefully and asked, "Taxi?"

"First time, eh?" the islander returned with a laugh.

"Excuse me?"

"Never been 'ere before?"

"No," David admitted, reluctantly.

"Where you headed?" pressed the grizzled presumptive gatekeeper.

David looked quickly at the handwritten envelope, still in his grasp. "163 Island Road."

The islander furrowed his brow, uncomprehending.

"Who's place?"

"Samuel Brown..."

The islander's amusement suddenly faded, replaced by a serious look. He hauled himself up to his full height and appraised David a bit more carefully. "Something about Dougie?"

David was astounded by this sudden change in demeanor. "Excuse me?"

"Doug Brown?" the islander quizzed. "You from the hospital? Insurance? ...or the police?"

David shook his head. "No; No, I just need to talk with..."

"If you're a salesman," the native interrupted, "I wouldn't be bothering these folks right now..."

David was now mildly irritated. "I'm not a salesman," he declared. "I'm Claire Winslow's son."

"Claire's son? Ya don't say..."

David's interest was suddenly piqued. "You knew my mother?"

"Sure! Everyone round here knows Claire! Knows 'bout her, anyway. Been a while... but I knew her, for sure."

"When did you last see her here?" David asked, trying to square this bold pronouncement, and it's maker, with the mother he knew.

"Oh, golly..." the stranger mussed. "We was kids, I'd

say… Teenagers…" The islander looked uncomfortable. "She was a Winthrop then…" He shifted his body weight as he scanned the parking lot. "Say!" he brightened. "I see John Brown over there; Let me get you a ride…"

~

The sky was a beautiful blue and the water reflected the same rich color, periodically reaching in like liquid fingers, wrapped around irregular protrusions of tall forested lands, sloping down from the traveled way. The winding country road, it's thick pavement just about wide enough for two vehicles to pass safely, had no break-down lane and shoulders that seemed to be several inches lower than the surface of the road.

John Brown's red pick-up truck rolled along, weaving through the outskirts of the village, out past the volunteer fire station and town garage, then on past the school house and Islander store. "Your grandmother's buried in there…" John noted, pointing out the Fuller Cemetery as they passed it on the curve.

Inside the cab, David sat buckled in the passenger seat, trying to get a handle on the driver, a mature sixty year old with a cowboy hat covering his thinning hair. John drove in a relaxed, casual manner, waving to drivers who were passing the other way. He had kept up a steady stream of commentary, pointing out various landmarks along the way that he thought might be of any slight interest to his captive audience.

David noted that the base of the cemetery gate looked to be about a foot lower than the roadway. Beyond the gate, the stones in the graveyard seemed to range from ancient slate to simple modern granite, with only a few massive granite and ornate marble memorials in sight. "So you really knew my mother?" he asked.

"I would *say* so…" John postured.

"Well, what can you tell me?" David queried. "How *well* do you remember her?"

"Oh, *real well*, that's for sure!" John blustered. "Why, she was here every Summer…" John paused for a moment. "Well, before the accident anyway…"

Ten

July 2, 1960

The sky was a brilliant blue, extending down to and blending seamlessly with the waters that surrounded the island. The few scattered clouds, that dared to float in from the West, reflected only in the sparkling waters of the Fresh Pond. The beautiful, thirteen year old Claire, her long, dark hair flowing, sat in the field at the top of the hill, weaving a delicate necklace of wild flowers as she sang:

"There's a summer place

Where it may rain or storm

Yet I'm safe and warm

For within that summer place

Your arms reach out to me

And my heart is free from all care

"For it knows

There are no gloomy skies

When seen through the eyes

Of those who are blessed with love

"And the sweet secret of

A summer place

Is that it's anywhere

Where two people share

All their hopes

All their dreams

All their love

"There's a summer place

Where it may rain or storm

Yet I'm safe and warm

In your arms, in your arms

In your arms, in your..."

At that moment, sixteen year old John Brown came running up the hill, his hands cupped together. He reached the top of the hill quickly, and plopped down beside Claire.

"Hey! Careful!" Claire exclaimed. "Don't squash my flowers!"

"Claire! Guess what I found?!!" John said excitedly, edging closer to Claire.

"In your hands?"

"Yes! You'll never guess!" he exclaimed, his eyes gleaming.

Claire scowled and cocked her head to the side. "Then why did you ask me to guess?"

John rolled his eyes, but he couldn't help smiling. He opened his hands and revealed an oyster with the shell cracked open. "Look!"

"A pearl?!!" Claire squealed, eyes open wide. "You found a pearl?!!"

John nodded his head and opened the shell halves to reveal a small, irregular pearl. "What do you think?!!"

"It's beautiful! Where did you find it?"

"Come on… I'll show you…"

John closed the shell halves and stuffed them in his pocket while Claire scooped up her flowers. They ran off, over the crest of the hill, down toward the old Carriage House and barn, on their way to the stone dam beyond.

Claire and John had been Summer friends for many years, in spite of their age difference, ever since the first time she had come upon him, alone, picking muscles off the rocks of the dam. "What are you doing on my rocks?" Claire had demanded, holding her hands on her little hips as only a five year old can do, her dark hair blowing wildly in the breeze.

John had squinted up at the source of the question to assess the situation before forming his response. "My grandfather put these rocks here," he had retorted, figuring that, at eight, he was smart enough to hold his own against this wispy little challenger. "Besides," he continued, his voice less defensive as he saw Claire thinking about what he had said, "these mussels are below the water line, so they don't belong to anyone in particular."

"Can you show me how to do that?" Claire had asked, sitting down and dangling her feet over the edge of the dam.

"Sure!" John had replied, and thus their friendship had begun. It existed only between the coming and going of the Summer ferry, never reaching out beyond the safe haven of their shared island. That was how it was, and that was just fine with all concerned.

As they started down the hill, Claire could see that old Hiram Brown was tending one of his regulars over by the woodshed, framed by the beautiful American Elm tree, planted many years before by John's great grandfather, Samuel. Claire didn't recognize the car, so she wasn't sure if the customer was one of the duPonts, or perhaps a Lamont, getting fresh produce for their dinner. Either way, it looked like a nice order, freshly washed and wrapped neatly in brown bags. She couldn't see his face clearly, but Claire knew old Mr. Brown was smiling as he exchanged pleasantries with his grateful customer.

Claire remembered fondly how he used to let her help pick peas from time to time, until, one day, he laughingly told her, "Miss Claire, I just can't *afford* to have you help me anymore!" It wasn't that he had ever paid her, exactly. It was her fondness for cracking open nearly every other pod she had picked so she could snack on the crisp, fresh peas, thus significantly reducing the inventory of his crop! She didn't argue that time; She knew how hard he worked to keep his gardens productive, and she loved his gentle spirit.

"Nice Woodie!" John exclaimed, appraising the fancy station wagon parked in front of the house, clearly more taken by that than thoughts of his aging grandfather.

They reached the bottom of the hill, just South of the big barn, as forty-four year old Samuel Brown was leading Bessie, the cow, through the big open doorway, into the stall area. His father's 1941 green Chevy pickup truck, with bales of hay in the truck bed, was parked next to the Carriage House.

"Hi, Mr. Brown!" Claire sang out as they approached the barn. "Are you going to milk Bessie again?"

"Hi, Dad…" said John, a bit less cheerfully.

"Don't be spooking Ole Bessie now…" Mr. Brown warned. "We don't want her giving us sour milk!"

Claire giggled. "You're so funny, Mr. Brown! Cows don't give sour milk!"

Sam Brown smiled. "You don't say…"

"Hey, Dad… Is it O.K. if we take the dinghy out for a while?"

"Can I milk her this time?" Claire asked with a bright smile.

"But, Claire…" John objected.

"Simmer down!" the farmer declared. "We all can't talk at the same time! Now, John Brown, the answer is 'No'… Randy took the dinghy down the Mill Stream with some friends."

"Why did Randy take *our* dinghy?" John asked with a frown.

"Because his mother took some of her friends out in their skiff to show off her new Cat boat. Anyway, I need you to help me finish up the chores so we can get out there and haul some traps before the storm rolls in later tonight... And you... 'No' to you, young lady."

"But, I really want to try it!..." Claire protested, "...and I *promise* I'll be gentle..."

"Well, that may be so," Samuel countered, looking down at Claire with some amusement, "but I can assure you your father won't be so gentle if Ole Bessie got agitated all of a sudden and decided to let you know it!"

"Oh, come on, Mr. Brown! Bessie won't hurt me!" Claire protested.

"That's exactly right!" Samuel declared triumphantly. "Now, if you want to help someone, I might suggest you run along back over to Sunnyside and see if you can help Mrs. Brown set the table for supper. Your folks are entertaining a gang of people over there and I am *quite* sure Mrs. Brown could use a helping hand or two..."

"Are you *sure* I can't help with Ole Bessie?..." Claire tried, one more time.

John sighed in resignation. "Come on, Claire..."

Sam Brown chuckled. "I appreciate the offer, but I'm standing my ground... Come along now, John. The hens need some tending..." he concluded, leading Bessie further into the barn, out of sight.

John took the oyster shells out of his pocket and offered them to Claire. "Here! You can have this..." John said solemnly, then he brightened right up. "Hey... Do you want to hike over to Mullen's Head tomorrow?"

"O.K.! Thanks!" Claire said, her face lit up as she accepted the gift, adding the shells to her collection of flowers. "When will you be done with your chores?"

"I'll get up early..." John promised, "and if it rains, I'll be free sooner! I'll come and get you, O.K.?"

"O.K.! See you tomorrow!"

John smiled and ran off, disappearing into the barn. Claire turned slowly and walked away, past the dung pile, toward the old farmhouse, carrying her flowers and oyster shells. She smiled and waived to Hiram Brown, now walking slowly toward the lettuce bed, box and knife in hand, his back arched permanently toward the ground. He stopped and sat back on his haunches for a moment so he could wave a greeting in return, a broad smile on his face, then he slowly returned to his question mark posture, determined to work until the last ray of sunshine.

It was only at that point that Claire noticed John's great uncle, Chester, sitting quietly in the shade of the two ancient apple trees that proudly marked the edge of the South yard. Chester was fifty-six years old, but could not read or write, and possessed limited cognitive skills. He worked hard along with his older brother, Hiram, doing exactly as he was told, though not always happily.

However well he was cared for – and it was clear that Hiram Brown was diligent and thoughtful in this regard – Claire had a strong sense that Uncle Chester must be very lonely in his protected little universe, especially during the long off season when she wasn't around. Come Summer, he was always ready to play croquet, caroms, marbles, or simple card games after his chores were done, no matter how long the work day had been. When she was younger, Claire had enjoyed many piggy-back rides through the fields, courtesy of Uncle Chester, and she, in turn, had helped him win every hand of Old Maids, always sitting to his left so she could draw the dreaded card from him, if need be. Claire often thought that Uncle Chester would have been less lonely if only he had been born fifty or so years later, when he would have had the opportunity to attend the special education programs at school, something that apparently didn't exist in 1904.

Claire jogged over to the apple trees. "Did you have a good day, Uncle Chester?" Claire asked, reaching out and gently touching his shoulder to get his attention. He didn't hear as well as he used to, she had noticed recently.

"It would be nice if you could visit me sometime," Chester responded, obviously not having heard Claire's question.

"Did you have a good day, Uncle Chester?" Claire repeated, smiling earnestly.

"I had to chop up some old trees out in the woods over there," he replied, pointing off to the South-East, toward a thick stand of trees by the pond. "then haul them over here to the woodshed," he concluded, shaking his head. "I don't know why Hidy makes me do that," he grumbled, uncharacteristically. "It was hot out there, and that old wood shed is plenty full."

"Well, it's nice and cool right here!" Claire observed, trying to cheer him up.

"Do you want to play some croquet?" he asked hopefully.

"How about after dinner?" Claire asked. "I promised John's dad I'd go help Elsie right now," she continued, pointing in the general direction of Sunnyside.

"It would be nice if you could visit me sometime and play a game of croquet," he answered sadly, clearly understanding that she was about to leave.

"Oh! Look what John found!" she said, holding out the oyster shells for him to see.

"Dirty old shells," he responded, making a face.

"No! It's a pearl!" Claire said, opening the shells so he could see better. "Isn't it pretty?" He scowled, looking hard at the shells, and Claire decided his vision must be fading as well. "See the flowers I found up the hill?" she asked, pulling the oyster back and holding up the unfinished necklace. She was determined to make him smile!

"Pretty flowers," he said, "Do you want to play a game of croquet?"

Claire smiled. "I promise I'll come back after dinner and we'll play then, O.K.?"

He smiled and started to push himself up from the chair. "I'll set it up."

"After dinner – *supper*," she said firmly, remembering that he had dinner at Noon. "After supper…"

"After supper," he repeated, standing up and pointing toward the woodshed. "I'll just go ahead and set it up."

Claire smiled. "O.K…. I promise I'll come back for a game as soon as I finish supper." She felt bad, wondering what he did when she wasn't around. She knew John had only so much patience with his great uncle. Chester smiled and walked slowly off to the woodshed to retrieve his croquet set, and Claire turned to get back on her way home.

She skipped down the rise that separated the old farmhouse from the road, then crossed to the gently curving driveway that sloped steeply down toward the stone dam. Claire had never known it to be anything other than a dam, but she had seen old pictures showing a bridge over this stretch of the Mill Stream, one capturing a much younger Hiram Brown crossing the partially submerged bridge in waders, apparently at the height of a full moon tide. Hiram had built the dam, stone by stone, creating a salt water pond that was affectionately known by the locals as Hidy's Pond.

On a gently sloping rise above Hidy's Pond sat a pretty white New England Farmhouse with a traditional kitchen ell, attached at the Eastern end to a two-story, natural shingle woodshed, connected on the South side by a farmer's porch that stretched the length of the ell. A medium sized red barn sat close by, to the South-East, converted recently to an oversized garage for Isabella Winthrop's fancy new Jaguar. The house and barn were framed by beautiful, flowering gardens, tended, Claire knew, by John's mother, Elsie. Named Sunny-side by Hiram Brown's mother, Attaresta "Attie" Brown, the name had stuck, long after the old home-stead had been sold to John Winthrop to cover her med-ical expenses.

~

Attie had, in fact, moved across the pond into Hiram's farmhouse with her simple minded son, Chester, seven years after her husband and two of her children had failed to survive a bout of influenza.

Hiram had actually moved to the mainland at age nine-teen and successfully completed school to become an accountant. He then moved on to Boston where he knew he could earn a better salary with his skills. Three years later, he came back to pay off his father's debts and to help his mother settle his father's estate. It was then, much like George Bailey, that Hiram discov-ered that his younger brother, Gerald, had been offered a good job in Augusta, working for his fiancée's father. His six other able siblings had already moved on with their lives, all seeking the greater opportunities offered on the mainland, just as had been his intentions. After a sleepless night weighing the options, Hiram accepted the need to move back to the island to take care of his mother.

Being a farmer had not been part of his dream, but he now became resigned to the fact that it was obviously his destiny. His father, Samuel, had, after all, tended him through the night when he was seventeen and delirious with fever, pressing cold compresses to his forehead, keeping a good supply of liquids nearby to ensure that his son was hydrated, and maintaining a vigil to see that he was continuously wrapped in warm blankets to ward off the chills. His father had fought for his life while his mother had lain sick in the next room, exhausted after tending Olive and Albert, her nine and twelve year old children who had already been stuck down by the dread disease. Samuel had saved his eldest son and given his life in exchange, falling deathly ill two days later, before his wife was well enough to nurse him.

How could Hiram not alter his life plans when his father's empty shoes loomed so large? Yes, he had come back to the island, settled down across the way from his mother's house, in his great grandfather's old homestead, and looked after his mother and brother. He had taken a wife, the fragile Elisa Stewart who had come to North Island, by some strange twist of fate, to teach the island children in the little one-room school house. Soon enough, the couple had presented Attie with a new grandson, named Samuel to honor her dead husband.

Elisa had not survived, unfortunately. The story was widely told, based entirely on Hiram's report, that during a stormy full moon tide, with the bridge washed out, she had accidentally capsized Hiram's old row boat and drowned while crossing the Mill Stream, intending to look in on her ailing mother-in-law. He had been at home, with little Samuel, having earlier soaked and exhausted himself through and through, down by the Fresh Pond, pulling a frightened old cow out of a ditch she had somehow stumbled into.

The cow part of the story was true. Elisa's death by drowning, however, had been no accident. In fact, had she not suffered a critical last minute surge of guilt, she would have taken her infant son with her, instead of leaving him at the old landing, squalling in a basket.

Hiram had not understood her lack of happiness and tender enthusiasm for her first born child. He had seen his own mother, all too often, either blissfully serene or puffed up with pride after giving birth to one of his many siblings. Postpartum depression was an unknown diagnosis in 1917, and Hiram was beside himself with bewilderment over what he perceived as his wife's sullen resentment of him and their child.

His bewilderment, however, turned quickly to terror, then grief, when he came home from the fields that stormy day to find the kitchen fire had gone cold. The note on the kitchen table, written neatly in Elisa's hand, stated the case plainly enough. She had decided, without reservation and in no uncertain terms, that she was ending her life and taking her infant son with her to spare him the misery of having to live on that desolate island. Racing down the hill to the landing in the blinding rain, frantically calling her name, Hiram had been overjoyed to hear his son's vigorous cries rising up the embankment.

He burned the note. Used it to kindle the kitchen fire that eventually dried their soggy clothing as he cradled his sleeping son, thankfully exhausted from all his crying. He never spoke of it, knowing it was a secret he was honor bound to keep. She had spared his son; He would spare her shame. He was a faithful secret keeper; He took it all to his grave.

When he found her body at low tide the next day, tangled in the reeds in one of the shallow coves at the end of the Mill Stream, he saw to it that she was taken care of properly and laid to rest up at the Fuller Cemetery, in a double plot, next to his father's grave.

His mother moved in to care for baby Samuel and to cook and clean for Hiram, keeping her son free to tend the rigors of the farm. Attie's move had not been conceived as a permanent one, but the untimely death of Hiram's young wife had had a catalytic effect, cementing the bond between mother, son, brother, and grandson that typified their strong New England heritage. Hiram had come back to the island, stayed, and looked after his mother and young brother, and now he was able to allow her to look after him and his infant son.

John Winthrop bought Attie's home several years later. Her breast cancer had been an unexpected blow, forcing Hiram to relinquish the home of his birth in order to provide the best possible care for his mother. The radical double mastectomy preserved Attie's life for a while, but in less than two years, Hiram was left alone again, with the responsibility of his adolescent son and Chester, his simple younger brother.

Although the sisters Leadbetter were regularly attentive over the years, dropping by in their Sunday finest to deliver home baked morsels that could easily best all the competition at the annual Grange fair, Hiram was never tempted to relieve either from their spinsterhood. He smiled and charmed them with his good humor, but he had no time or inclination to try marriage again.

When government regulations on meat production cut sharply into the profits he could realize from his long-standing husbandry practice, his flock of sheep and most of his cattle were sold to a mainlander, and Hiram was forced to sell his remaining lands to the Winthrops, retaining life estate for himself, his brother, and his son.

Samuel, handsome and hard working by anyone's standards, and newly engaged to marry the striking Elsie

Witherspoon, had been hired by the elder Mr. Winthrop as caretaker, a job he would hold for life. After their marriage, Elsie had moved right in and picked up where Attie had left off, taking care of the Brown men and cooking and cleaning for the Winthrops.

~

As she crossed the dam that late afternoon in 1960, Claire noticed that there were several shiny 1958 - 1960 model vehicles parked by the barn, next to her father's 1950 Desoto Custom, obvious proof that the new ferry was, indeed, making it easy for friends to visit the island. There was a small group of people, in semi-casual Summer attire, laughing and playing croquet in the yard, additional confirmation that Mr. Brown's assertions about her parents entertaining guests were quite correct.

Claire continued up the long driveway, smiling in acknowledgement of several adults, sitting in the bright red Adirondack chairs in front of the South garden, then she quickly disappeared into the kitchen ell, in search of Elsie Brown.

Her eyes had been on Sunnyside, and, completely out of character, she had not looked down stream even once when she crossed the dam. If she had, Claire would have noticed that the blue of the sky off to the West was now fringed by heavy clouds and a rolling thick fog.

Eleven

November 28, 2006

John Brown's red pick-up truck continued to roll along Island Road, at an amazingly leisurely pace, while John recounted his memories of Claire to her son, waving at every passing car, though David suspected he didn't know each and every person.

"Yep... Sweet as they come, Claire was..." John summarized, shaking his head. "Quite a shock, how she died..." His voice trailed off as he looked to the left at the tip of a harbor. "I still can't hardly believe it; A tragic accident, just like her mother..." he concluded, shaking his head.

David wrinkled his brow in thought for a moment. "What exactly happened to her mother?" he asked, realizing that John was a font of information.

"Got rammed by a boat out there in Pulpit Harbor," he replied, nodding his head toward the water.

Twelve

July 2, 1960

Thirty-six year old Isabella Winthrop sat at the helm of her Beetle Cat boat, fussing with the sail which was luffing in an almost dead calm. She had not planned to cruise anywhere today, with so many guests to entertain, but Randolph had promised Sarah and Richard a "sample" cruise if they ever came to visit, and they had chosen that very day to make good on their talk. That convenient new ferry had a down side, after all!

Now Isabella sat with her friends, becalmed somewhere in the waters of outer Pulpit Harbor, with a thick fog quickly rolling in around them, and a house full of guests back at Sunnyside. Elsie was there preparing dinner; Nothing to worry about on that score. Her dress was all laid out so she could change quickly when she got back from this little escapade; No problem there. She couldn't do anything to alter the freakish weather conditions, so Isabella sat and smiled at Sarah and Richard. She shook her head, but her smile remained on her beautiful face. "I can't believe this! What happened to our magnificent day?"

"What happened to our wind!" exclaimed Sarah.

Isabella had stopped struggling with the sail for a moment and looked around as wisps of fog seemed to reach out toward the little boat. "This fog is thick as pea soup!" she said with a scowl. "I think it just absorbed all the air in the harbor!"

Sarah's husband, Richard, trying to be helpful, started looking in the storage compartments of the small boat. "Do we have any lights?"

"No…" sighed Isabella, her frown quickly turning into a weak smile. "Not unless Elsie was clever enough to pack a flash light in the lunch basket with the sandwiches!"

"Do we have oars?" Sarah asked hopefully.

"Did anyone think to take them out of the dinghy?" Isabella asked, looking quickly around the deck, berating herself silently for having been so careless. Going out on short notice was no excuse for reckless conduct. She was quietly embarrassed by her lack of forethought.

Sarah sighed and shook her head. "Well… Never let it be said that you don't know how to show your friends a good time!"

"Very funny!" Isabella retorted with a smile. She stood up straight and peered into the fog. "Don't worry… The wind will pick up…"

Suddenly a power boat broke through the fog and rammed the Cat boat. Sarah grabbed onto Richard and they were thrown to the deck, wedged against the side of the boat, but Isabella was cast overboard by the force of the blow, disappearing immediately into the bay as the fog closed quickly around the stricken vessel.

Thirteen

November 28, 2006

John Brown took a sharp turn up a long gravel drive-way. "What a fuss!" he exclaimed, shaking his head. "Just about everyone was out there trying to find her! Took near about two full weeks before the poor woman was hauled out – by my Dad, don't you know." He paused, thinking back in time. "Went out after supper to haul a few traps, and there she was! All tangled up!"

He looked at David and furrowed his brow. "Came up with them Northern Lights, real spooky like…" he said with a little shiver. "If my dad was a drinking man he might have dropped her back in, but he knew right away what it was and kept a real cool head about himself…"

He paused a beat and pointed to a pretty New England Farmhouse, a short distance away, with several out-buildings, sitting on a rise beyond a body of water, accessed by a long, winding driveway running over a stone dam. "That's Sunnyside, across the way…"

He took a deep breath and continued almost wistfully, "Yep; Every Summer, just like clockwork, Claire and all the Winthrops gathered over there… Yes sir; Lots and lots of memories…"

David looked out the window and wondered aloud, "Who owns it now?"

"Why, old Randolph – Mr. Winthrop" John asserted, "held on to her all this time…"

"My grandfather?"

"I would say so…"

"So he still comes here?"

"Oh, God no!" John assured his passenger. "Been years since he come here! I mean, he kept coming for a spell after the accident, but when Randy got shot down over in Nam, well… I guess he kind of died right along with him. Buried him next to Mrs. Winthrop – back there at Fuller – and never came back, that I know of, after that."

David took another hard look at the distant home. "So nobody lives there?"

"Well…" John mussed, "she set empty, don't you know, for a number of years before he decided to have my folks rent it out for him."

"What about my mother?"

"Well, now…" John said, scratching his head for a moment. "Claire stopped coming pretty much after her mother's accident… Hard to figure…"

"What do you mean?"

"Well, hard to figure why she never came back; I mean, she *loved* it here! Talked like there was no place better in the whole wide world!"

David thought about it for a few moments. "Maybe it made her think about her mother's accident?"

"Could be..." John answered thoughtfully. "I don't know... Her mom's death was a mighty tragic accident, I'll admit, but, like I said, Randy and old Mr. Winthrop kept coming back after the accident... I don't know why she just gave us the heave-ho, more or less."

David looked sharply back at John. "But my Dad says Mother was always involved with your family..."

"Oh, don't get me wrong, now!" John protested immediately. "Claire's been mighty good to my folks all these years," he assured David. "I just don't get why she stopped coming... Course, I went away to school and all, so I didn't really get to talk with Claire after that Summer, but I am the *most* surprised person that she just never came back..."

"And your brother?"

"My brother?" John asked, as if surprised by the question. "Dougie? Oh, he wasn't even born then..."

David shrugged his shoulders. "Well, what can you tell me about him?"

"Dougie? I don't hardly know what to say about that boy..."

"He's forty-five!" David responded with a hint of irritation.

"Well, I'm sixty," John countered, "so I guess you could say we weren't exactly growing up together."

"But, he's your brother!"

"Well, sure, but that don't necessarily mean nothing…" John continued. "We never really lived together, so I don't guess I know him all that well. I mean, Mom had him when I was off at trade school. I went away being an only son and came home to find this screaming little baby all of a sudden has taken over the house!"

"You didn't know your mother was pregnant?" David asked, surprise registering in his voice.

"Not a hint!" John replied emphatically. "Old Yankees, that's all, keeping private business to themselves. Here we are…"

John's red truck pulled up the driveway and parked alongside a 1941 Chevy pick-up with a valid license plate on the back.

"Your dad's truck?" David asked, impressed by the condition of the old truck.

"You bet!" John said with some pride. "Old Yankees, like I said… My grandfather bought it new in 1941. Dad keeps that thing running one way or the other! Eighty-nine now and my dad still changes his own oil, now and again…"

Samuel Brown, a slight, thin, elderly man walked by wearing a heavy jacket and a broad brimmed hat, carrying something in a bucket. A yellow cat followed him closely. He smiled and nodded to John but kept walking, intent on his mission.

John smiled, nodded his head, and waved to Samuel. "Doesn't hear very well now, though…"

~

Inside the barn-style home, eighty-five years old Elsie Brown was busy baking. A pleasant, sturdy woman, she took a baking sheet out of the oven and looked up in surprise as John opened the front door. She brushed loose strands of hair away from her smiling face. "John! What a nice surprise! I wasn't expecting you, but I've got some fresh cookies here, right out of the oven!"

John lumbered into the kitchen, taking his hat off, a big smile on his face. David hesitated, but followed John into the house, closing the door behind him. Uncomfortable, he lingered, unnoticed, in the foyer area.

John zeroed in on the plate of fresh baked cookies. "Well now, there you go! I was down at the ferry and thought I could smell something good cooking *all* the way up here!" He picked up a fresh baked ginger snap and sampled it. "De-eee-licious!" he pronounced with a flourish, then he gave his mother a big hug and a kiss on the cheek. "Mom, this here is Claire's boy…"

"David… David Winslow…" David said, stepping forward to offer his hand.

Elsie's eyes filled with tears. "Oh… David… You've grown so big!..." She said as grasped David's hand. "My heart just breaks about your mother…" She paused and dabbed at the tears in the corners her eyes. "A terrible accident…"

"Thank you… I know you must be upset about your son being in a coma, but…" David shifted, feeling suddenly awkward. "…I don't understand why he was driving my mother's car, let alone driving so fast, and I thought you could help me with that."

Elsie blinked away tears as she looked hard into David's eyes. "I… I really couldn't say…"

John stepped forward and put a defensive arm around his mother. "Hold on, now!" he said with authority. "That's quite enough! There's no need to make her feel worse than she does already! Mom loved Claire, and right now she doesn't even know if her son is going to make it!"

Elsie patted John's arm. "It's O.K., son…"

"I'm sorry…" David said, looking at Elsie. "I don't mean any offense, but can you tell me why your son was even there? Or why my mother felt she had to take him under her wing like she apparently did?"

Elsie looked down, tears streaming from her eyes, and absently rubbed John's arm. "It was a terrible accident…"

John took a step toward David. "That's enough! I think it best you leave now…"

"No, no…" countered Elsie, trying to soothe her agitated son. "It's O.K.…."

David glanced at John then looked apologetically at Elsie. "I just want to know why your son was driving Mother's car…"

John lost his patience. "Mom had nothing to do with that!"

"It's O.K., John..." Elsie quickly asserted. "He means no harm..."

David shook his head, taking two steps back. "I don't... I'm sorry..."

Elsie took a deep breath and looked at David sadly. "I can't tell you anything... I just can't..."

"Satisfied?" John snapped. "She can't tell you anything you don't know already..."

"It's O.K., son..."

"It's not O.K.!" John insisted. "He's got no right get-ting' you all riled up just because Claire handed the darn keys to Dougie! You can't be expected to under-stand why she did it! It was an accident! Nothing more! If he wants to know all the particulars, he can just wait 'till Dougie wakes up..."

"It's O.K., really..." Elsie said in a soothing manner as she stepped toward David and reached out to touch his hand again. "I know you just miss your beautiful mother... Such a sweet, caring soul... I don't blame you for being hurt and angry, but I really can't tell you what you want to know... I'm sorry..."

Fighting his emotions, David locked eyes with a sym-pathetic Elsie, tears glistening on her cheeks and pour-ing in his heart.

～

David left the barn house alone and wandered down the hill, looking critically at the old farmhouse and trying to imagine his mother ever being happy here. It made no sense, yet David's instincts told him it was all too true. Why, then, had she kept this place such a secret?

He stopped at the top of a knoll to gaze across at the beautiful farmhouse called Sunnyside. It was clearly in much better condition that the old farmhouse on this side of the pond, but he still struggled to imagine his mother inhabiting such a place.

He started to turn away when a movement in the tall grass, much further down the hill, across the road, caught his attention. David squinted his eyes, unsure about what he was seeing. It was, in fact, thirteen year old Olivia Brown, running after her puppy, but David could barely see her and certainly had no idea who she was.

A white truck suddenly came into view and pulled up to a stop at the top of the drive running down to the dam. David could see that the truck was being driven by someone with long red hair. Unable to actually pull off the road, the driver simply beeped the horn until the young dark haired girl came running up the hill to the truck, her puppy in her arms, and quickly got into the passenger seat.

As the truck drove away, David got only a glimpse of the red haired woman behind the wheel, but could not make out the features of the young girl. David stood there with a puzzled expression on his face, thinking that he had seen this young girl before, though he could not quite place her, or the red haired driver.

His thoughts were broken by the sound of an engine coming up behind him. David turned to see John Brown pull up in his red truck. "You better hop in..." John yelled out the window, his face no longer wearing a welcoming mask. "You don't want to miss the ferry..."

Fourteen

November 30, 2006

The Westport Police Station was located in the center of town, just to the right of the Town Hall. David and Anne had made the fifteen minute trip to Central Village, ostensibly to pick up some coffee rolls from Perry's Bakery, but David had decided to stop by the Police Station to talk with Chief Macomber.

"I'm sorry, son," the amiable Police Chief said, shaking his head and doing his best to be sympathetic. "Honest to God, I am... But I can't press charges – even if I *thought* I knew what happened – so long as the poor guy is in a coma."

"Poor guy!" David exploded. "He killed my mother!" Anne stood anxiously beside him, her hand lightly touching his back, as if ready to hold him back.

"Now, just calm down!" Chief Macomber cautioned, his facade of kindness quickly evaporating. "You know perfectly well what I mean! It's just an expression... O.K.?" He paused and took a deep breath, trying to soften his stern look. "Your mother was a fine, civic minded woman," he continued, "and I promise you, we want to get to the bottom of this just as much as you do. We don't want to have this dragging on any longer than is absolutely necessary, but this is an *accident* investigation, and I am not taking any shortcuts; O.K.?" He paused to assess the impact of his words before pressing on. "Now, we know there was no alcohol involved, but we don't know if there was some kind of mechanical failure that caused the car to speed out of control."

"*Ninety* miles an hour?" David rejoined skeptically.

"Son! Just settle down and let me do my job! Have I made myself clear?"

~

In spite of Anne's rigorous objections, David drove past Adamsville Road, turned left on Hixbridge Road, and then headed North on Route 88, determined to drive to the hospital in Providence, a drive that was marked by infrequent, terse exchanges.

They had never really fought about anything in the six years they had known each other, and it seemed both tragic and incomprehensible to Anne that they were, at this crucial point in time, unable to discuss this particular situation calmly and rationally, as they had so many other things over the years. She had been more than supportive since the accident, but it seemed to her that David was, step by step, losing his perspective completely on this subject, and, for the very first time in their relationship, he was not being even marginally receptive to her point of view.

Thirty minutes later, David and Anne walked through the hospital's main entrance and approached the information desk, silence now cementing the bond between them. An elderly receptionist sat behind the counter. "Excuse me," David asked softly, "Douglas Brown? Can you tell me what room he's in?"

The receptionist looked at the computer on her desk. "Douglas Brown? Let me see..." she murmured as she scanned her computer screen. "O.K.; Here he is; Are you family?" she asked, without looking up from the screen.

David did a quick double take before responding, "Yes; Brother; John Brown," he said, squeezing Anne's hand, trusting that, in spite of her pique, she would not give him away.

"Room 402," the receptionist said, finally looking back at David, "directly opposite the nurse's station; Take the elevator to the fourth floor and turn right, through the double doors."

The busy hospital corridor felt sterile and impersonal as David and Anne walked slowly, wordlessly, making their way to Room 402. Finding it, they entered and found Douglas Brown lying rigid, tubes running to several different bags of fluids, hung high above his bed, and monitors blinking and beeping, off to the right. David stopped just through the threshold, frozen in his tracks, conflict and disappointment clearly evident in his eyes. Anne said nothing, but she really wanted to say, "I told you so…".

~

The little black sports car pulled up the driveway in Westport, quickly coming to a full stop, and David and Anne spilled out immediately, continuing their argument in hushed tones. "I can't believe you're making such a big deal out of this!" David hissed, shrugging his shoulders. "How did I hurt anyone?"

Anne shook her head in exasperation. "Well… You lied, for one thing!"

"I didn't think she would give me the room number if she thought I wasn't a family member!" David protested.

"So, now you think it's O.K. to lie to get what you want? And what did it end up getting you?

David shook his head. "One lie! Stop making such a big deal about it!"

Anne closed her eyes for a moment, as if asking for some divine intervention. "But, what are you doing, David?" she asked, fixing her stare back on him. "What do you think you are going to accomplish, poking around like this? Compromising your integrity?"

David rolled his eyes. She was right, but he didn't want to hear her. "There's something missing – don't you get that?" he asked in answer to her question. "There's something about this guy that just doesn't fit!"

"Well, let the police figure it out! That's their job!"

"You just don't understand!"

"I understand perfectly!" Anne replied, her voice rising in frustration. "I think *you* don't realize how obsessed you've become!" She took a deep breath and tried to reign in her emotions. "Don't *you* understand that by running around like some kind of *vigilante* detective, you are *not* going to change things!" she continued, her voice softened dramatically. "It's not going to bring her back, and it's not going to help you move on and get back to living your own life!"

David paused and looked out past the house toward the open bay. "I *need* to understand…" he said, turning to walk away, toward the guest house.

"Where are you going?" Anne demanded, perplexed by his actions.

David paused and responded, "I want to take a look around," never once looking directly at Anne.

Anne shook her head and turned toward the front door. "I'm going inside…"

~

David walked, alone, over to the small Cape style structure, separated from the Winslow home by a fine gravel driveway. A red pick-up truck, with Maine tags, sat just outside the door. David hesitated, then entered the guest house.

Inside, everything was neat and in good order, just as his mother had set it up years ago. Architectural plans for the kitchen expansion were laid out on the desk, in front of the picture window. David walked over to the desk and unrolled another set of architectural plans. Puzzled at first, he finally realized that they were clearly for the restoration of the old island farmhouse. He was taken aback for a moment when he noticed that the corner bedroom was identified as "David's Bedroom" and the middle room as "Amie's Bedroom".

David rolled up the plans and walked back outside, taking them with him. He stopped by the truck, paused, then opened the driver's door. He hesitated again, then got into the truck.

He sat in the driver's seat for a minute, as if hoping to *feel* something about the owner. Failing that, David looked around and noticed an envelope tucked above the visor. He pulled it out and saw that it had a stamp in the corner and was addressed to Elsie Brown. He turned it over and looked at it closely, then got out of the truck holding the sealed envelope in his hand, along with the rolled up architectural plans.

~

David entered the Post Office, clutching the stamped envelope. He started to drop it in the outgoing mail slot, then changed his mind at the last minute. He stepped back and pulled two wrinkled envelopes from his pocket.

Searching, he quickly found the same box number he had seen on the envelopes addressed to his mother. Fishing his mother's keys out of his pocket, he hesitated momentarily, then put the mail box key in the lock, turned the key, and pulled the little square door open. Looking inside, he was surprised to find two more envelopes sitting in the box. He slowly pulled them out, breathing deeply as he saw they were both from the Assessor's Office from the Town of North Island, and appeared to be official tax documents.

~

David burst into the Winslow home, clutching a handful of envelopes. Walking briskly into the den, he sat at the desk, opening the wrinkled envelope from Attorney Strong, setting the others aside on the green blotter. As he dialed the number on the letterhead, he unconsciously started tapping his foot on the floor.

Anne suddenly walked into the room and looked at David's angry face. "What's wrong?" she asked, raising her eyebrows quizzically.

"I just..." David gestured for Anne to be quiet, then he turned away from Anne and talked into the phone. "Attorney Strong please... David Winslow... Thank you..."

David waited impatiently. "Attorney Strong?" he finally said, breaking his stony silence. "My mother *owns* the Brown's home? You could have *at least* told me that!" he fumed. "Being a matter of public record, I can't believe you would consider this *privileged* information..."

Fifteen

The sky was a blend of near black and bright red, streaked with bold splashes of yellow-orange and pink. It flew by, punctuated by boulders – blurred gray impressions of boulders really – off to the right, flashing by like a strobe light, illuminated by the headlamps of the car.

Claire was sitting in the passenger seat of her treasured Jaguar, a look of terror frozen on her face. Her arms were outstretched, her left hand braced on the dashboard and her right hand gripping the door armrest, her head turned, as if to avoid seeing the great rocks flashing by. She opened her mouth but no sound came out as the car suddenly crashed into one of the boulders and folded into her... turning everything black.

~

"No!!!"

Anne rolled toward David who was lying on his back, hands gripping a section of the sheet and blanket, both hands clamped tightly. She struggled to wake up. "David... The dream again?"

David shook his head slowly, as he continued to look at the ceiling. "It's so hard to imagine what she must have felt..."

Anne didn't move. "It was just that dream again..."

"She must have been so scared..."

"Try not to think about it…"

"It just makes no sense…"

Anne could think of nothing more to say, so she rolled back over, wearily, and stared out the window on the opposite wall. The window revealed nothing, being full of darkness only, so, in truth, her eyes held fast to nothing in particular, except the tears glistening on their gently rounded surfaces, stubbornly refusing to fall.

~

It was a cloudy morning, both outside and in. Peter had left the house quite early, planning to park the car in Providence and take the train to New York. David sat alone in the morning room, a cup of coffee in hand, watching as the thick bank of clouds slowly brightened somewhat, while stubbornly holding back the rays of the sun.

Anne was sill upstairs, packing.

~

David lugged the suitcase out to Anne's car and lifted it into the trunk, popped open a few minutes earlier by Anne, her remote quietly doing the job from the bedroom window, mechanically efficient and suffering no second thoughts. She emerged from the home moments later and put her laptop and a few other smaller items in the back seat. David closed the trunk slowly but firmly and watched Anne for a moment, in silence, feeling unsettled by the tension that had clearly grown between them.

He took a deep breath and approached Anne, trying to force a smile. "Are you *sure* you can't stay a little longer?"

Anne shook her head. "I can't..."

"I'm sorry..."

Anne reached out suddenly and grabbed David's arm, her touch firm, yet gentle. "Come back with me..." she said, eyes pleading.

He shook his head. "I can't..."

"Yale would be so good for you right now..." Anne persisted.

"I can't just yet..."

"Yes you can!" Anne insisted. "If you would just force yourself to focus on something else! If you make an effort to try to get back into your studies, I know it would help!" She looked around, then turned back to him. "You're too close to this whole thing right now to get a good perspective," she continued urgently. "Just promise me you'll think about it..."

David stood a little taller and shook his head again. "Do you remember what happened on 9/11?"

"Of course..."

"Do you really *remember*?" David pressed. "I was *in* Manhattan on 9/11... I was scheduled to interview for that internship at Cantor Fitzgerald later that morning..." He shook his head, remembering. "I *saw* the towers fall!" He took a deep breath, reliving the horrible moment, as vividly as if it had just happened.

"I was standing on the rooftop of my building... and *watched* as the *towers* collapsed into a pile of rubble! The *World Trade Center* – a sight I *loved* – just *crumbled* to the earth in – what? – a minute?" David shook his head, closing his eyes momentarily. "Completely gone! Replaced by billowing towers of smoke and ash and hundreds or thousands of dead and injured people..."

"I know, but..."

"I had pointed them out to my Dad – just *two* days earlier – looking down the river toward the towers..." David shook his head and kept going down his dark memory lane, not hearing Anne, though he saw her lips moving. "I told him it was my *favorite* view in New York; In less than forty-eight hours, it was *gone* forever..."

Anne shrugged her shoulders. "I know all that, David, but I don't see..."

"They evacuated my neighborhood – I had just moved in!" David continued, seemingly not listening to Anne. "I walked for miles – with *thousands* of people – over the bridge, into New Jersey..." He shook his head again, then looked directly at Anne. "I had no place to stay that night, so I shared a hotel room with strangers..." he remembered, shaking his head. "I didn't know them, but they were in the same situation and could not have been kinder." David sighed. "The next morning, I took a bus up to New Haven, thinking I would feel 'normal' or at least *safer* there." He shook his head and looked off toward the ocean. "But they didn't *get* it..."

"I was *there*, David..." Anne interjected forcefully. "We were all *well* aware of what had happened in New York..."

David turned back to look at Anne. "But it didn't make a real *difference*!" he insisted. "Life went on there like nothing was wrong! Friends were like 'Wow! What an awful thing! Must have been awesome to see! Good thing your interview was scheduled for 11:00 or you might have been in the towers... Hey, there's a party at Tony's...' Like *nothing* happened!"

"Well, they didn't experience it like you did, David! They just had a different perspective..."

"*Exactly*!" David grabbed Anne's arms for emphasis. "My *whole world* was changed, but it was like Connecticut was on a different planet! My friends around there never even came close to grasping the real significance of 9/11..."

"O.K., but..."

"Don't you see, Anne? My *whole world* is changed – *again* – and I can't do New Haven right now! I don't *want* to!" David took a step closer and lowered his voice. "I can't understand why my mother is dead, and I can't walk around pretending that it doesn't matter..."

"Of course it matters!" Anne responded quickly, just short of anger. "Of course I get it! But you can't just stop living! Your mother would be the *first* to tell that – and you *know* I'm right!"

David shook his head. "When he wakes up... If I can

just talk with him for five minutes…"

"Doug Brown?" Anne queried. "And, what if he doesn't? What if he never wakes up? He's the only person alive who *really* knows what happened, David. If he *never* wakes up, are you going to suspend your whole life indefinitely, trying to figure it out?"

"No! No!" David took a step back, shaking his head vigorously. "I'm *sure* he'll wake up, and then I'll know; I just need to talk with him…"

"And what if he wakes up but doesn't remember anything?"

"He'll remember!"

Anne closed her eyes for a moment, shaking her head slightly, then looked directly into David's eyes. "And what about me?"

"What do you mean?"

Anne averted her eyes for a moment, head down, turned slightly away.

David softened his tone. "Anne… Come on…"

Anne looked at the engagement ring on her left hand, then slowly slid it off her finger. She looked at David, tears in her eyes, as she forced the ring into his hand. "I can't keep doing this…"

"Anne, please…" David stepped closer to Anne and touched her arm gently.

Anne looked at him with tears in her eyes. "I love you,

David..."

"Don't do this..." David pleaded, now gripping both of her arms.

Anne closed her eyes for a moment, and continued as if he hadn't spoken. "...but I can't watch you let this obsession take over your life..."

"Please, Anne..."

Anne took a deep breath and looked David in the eye, "...to the exclusion of everything... and everyone..."

David pulled Anne toward him and put his arms around her, holding her tight. Slowly, she extricated herself from the embrace and got into the car. It seemed like an eternity as she started the car and drove away, tears streaming down her face, while David stood in the driveway, watching.

Sixteen

December 2, 2006

David woke up on Saturday morning knowing exactly what he would do. He had debated with himself all day about driving to New Haven to try and patch things up with Anne, but when she didn't answer her cell phone after repeated calls, he decided that his original plan was his best course of action.

Up well before dawn, he brewed a pot of coffee, wrote a quick note to his father, filled a thermos, grabbed some fruit, and hit the road before Alice arrived to make breakfast.

Five hours later, David pulled into the ferry terminal parking lot in Rockland, a scant fifteen minutes before the first boat was scheduled to leave. He parked behind a big van, noting, as he quickly got out of the car, that his was the eighth vehicle in line, but that there were four big cars and one truck in the reservation queue and several big trucks ahead of him.

Running inside the terminal, David hurried over to the ticket window for the North Island ferry. "Round trip, please..."

The clerk looked at him with uncertainty. "One passenger?"

David paused and glanced back at the ferry schedule in his hand. "Car and driver..." he responded. "Do you think I'll make it on O.K.?" he asked turning to point out his place at the curve in the long line.

~

Thankfully, his car was small enough that the ferry crew had managed to stuff it in the forward left hand corner of the bow, pinning it by several larger vehicles, leaving less than ten inches to spare. David had not wasted any time inside the terminal, so he now squeezed out of his car and worked his way back to the head at the stern end of the cabin, glad to have the opportunity for some relief after the intensity of his non-stop drive.

He washed his hands and made his way back to his car just as the ferry started to move away from the dock. The sky was clear at the moment, but, looking out into the harbor, David saw the horizon cloaked in the puffy gauze of a thick, rolling bank of fog, obliterating the islands beyond.

He settled back in his car and looked around for something to read, grateful to find his dog-eared copy of Doris Kerns Goodwin's "Team of Rivals" on the shelf behind his seat. The book fell open to Chapter 22, "Still in Wild Water" and, with a momentary smile and Spinoza-like acceptance, David started to read about the Ohio and Pennsylvania elections of 1863. In spite of the fact that the tightly packed deck and the thick fog had eliminated most external distractions, David struggled to keep his focus on the political posturing of Salmon Chase and the continuing friction between him and William Seward. He was shaken to his core, however, and completely unable to concentrate on the written words beyond the point that Seward proposed to Abraham Lincoln that he should declare Thanksgiving Day a national holiday on the last Thursday of November, commending to God's care "all those who have become widows, orphans, mourners, or sufferers".

Blinking furiously to ward off a flood of emotion, David looked up and focused intently on the tiny droplets of moisture that had been deposited on his windshield as the gossamer coils of fog tumbled over the open deck. Dropping the book in the passenger seat, he opened his door and squeezed out again, moving, this time, toward the chain "gate" that was strung across the bow. He could see nothing, save for the water breaking on the bow, but the nothingness was comforting, and he let his mind go fully there.

~

In time, the fuzzy golden orb of the sun appeared, slowly becoming less distorted as the ferry finally passed through the bank of fog, entering the Thoroughfare. Patches of blue sky could be seen as the fog disappeared, gradually revealing the charming wooden structures of the tiny seaside village.

The ferry docked and, as the ramp was being lowered, David got back in his car and started the engine, his mind now set back on his mission. With the confidence of an old hand, he drove off a few moments later, turning right out of the parking lot and onto Main Road, then left, up the hill by Calderwood Hall.

~

Ten minutes later, David pulled into the parking space next to the 1941 Chevy pickup. He got out of the car and walked slowly to the front door, looking around at the simple beauty, here at the center of the island.

Inside the barn-style house, Elsie was just in the process of making a cup of tea when she heard the doorbell ring. She put down her old copper kettle and walked to the front door, expecting Samuel to be waiting there with an armload of kindling. She was stunned when she opened it and saw David standing there instead, an uncomfortable, weak smile on his face and an envelope in his hand.

~

Twenty minutes later, David was sitting at the table in the Morning room, a fresh cup of coffee and a plate of scrambled eggs in front of him. "You have to try it with molasses!" Elsie had insisted, so the dark, gooey syrup had been drizzled over the fluffy yellow pile.

"Mmmmmm… This is good!" David had to admit after one mouthful. "My mother used to eat this?" he asked, incredulously.

Elsie sat opposite him now, slowly removing a tea bag from her cup. "Yes, indeed!" she beamed, her mind quickly going back what seemed like centuries. The envelope David had brought sat on the table, next to a folded page. It caught Elsie's eye and her smile faded. "Thank you for bringing this…" Elsie said, her hand gently tapping the letter. "It would have been hard, I think, to get it in the regular mail…"

"You're welcome," David answered sincerely, swallowing another mouthful of eggs. "I felt bad that I was…" David shifted uncomfortably in his seat. "Well, I'm really sorry that I upset you last time…"

"No, please!" Elsie protested. "You don't need to apologize…"

David took a sip of coffee and was reflective for a moment. "I didn't really *plan* to come back, but when I found this letter… Well, I…" He paused and absently picked up his fork, then looked directly at Elsie. "I *also* discovered that my mother *owns* this property…"

Elsie leaned back in her chair, looking out the window as David waited, a forkful of eggs suspended over his plate. "Oh, dear… Yes I suppose so…"

David put down his fork. "You sound a little… uncertain…"

Elsie shook her head as she took a deep breath, letting it out with a sigh. She looked back at David, her eyes wide with concern, just short of fear. "I just never thought about it," she said softly. "It was going to be temporary…" She took another deep breath. "Oh, my! I guess that might be a bit of a problem now…"

"Please… Please don't worry, Mrs. Brown. I'm sure we can sort everything out," David said kindly, "But, I'm still a little confused…" he mused, pausing thoughtfully while he took a sip of coffee. "There are *two* deeds… My mother got *two* tax bills in the mail this week, and her lawyer has *two* deeds…"

"Her lawyer? Well…" Elsie paused and looked out the window. "I know that Claire and Sam worked it all out…" She looked down and took a sip of tea, then looked back at David with a hint of tears in her eyes. "Those darn taxes kept going up and up and up! Sam and I were struggling not to lose everything!" Elsie shook her head. "All our years living here… Just didn't seem right! But, Claire, God bless her! She kept us from having to sell the place, or being kicked off our land." She dabbed at the corner of her eye before continuing. "We *could* have sold the place, you know, but where would we go? Sam has lived here forever – born right down there in that old farmhouse – and he would just up and die if he had to leave the island..."

"I understand that," David responded sympathetically, "But, why are there two separate deeds?" he pressed.

"Oh..." Elsie said, leaning back in her chair as she thought back in time. "Well, I guess she had to split off a piece of land so she could have Dougie build this place..." Elsie looked around the room. "He did a nice job!" She looked back at David. "With all our money going to taxes, we just couldn't keep everything up, you know; The old farmhouse was falling apart – built in 1830 – and... well... Claire had a notion to build a *new* barn like the *old* one that blew down, back in '91, I think." Her tone shifted to one of sharing a great confidence. "She used to like to hang around out there when Sam was tending Ole Bessie – that was our cow's name — Well... a few of our cows had that name, I guess..."

Elsie realized she was wandering and shook her head and shoulders as if to get her thoughts back on track. She took a sip of tea and looked around again. "Yes, she sketched up a new barn – except it was for us people – and she hired Dougie to build it; He did a good job... Your mother saw that he had good training, though I think she would have been happier if Douglas really wanted to go to college..."

"Why?..." David interrupted, a puzzled look on his face. "What difference did it make to her?"

Elsie looked flustered. "Oh... Well... I think Claire just

believed he was so smart… you know… Like he could do more…"

"What did my mother have to do with any of that?"

"Oh… Well…" Elsie looked down as she took a sip of tea and gathered her thoughts. "Mr. Winthrop – your grandfather — he saw that our John got his education – became an electrician, he did!" she pronounced with a smile. "Of course, he does a bit of lobstering too, but no caretaking for that boy!" She nodded her head in approval, then her smile faded quickly. "Well… In the same way, you know… Claire saw to Dougie's education…"

Elsie looked down at her tea cup as her words fell off. David absorbed this information and was eager to find out more, but something told him that he had pressed Elsie enough for one day. He smiled, almost apologetically, and looked around the room, his gaze resting on the beautiful scene beyond the window. "This is so strange…" he commented softly. "I mean, my whole life, we never came here! But somehow my mother seems to have been deeply involved in all your lives…"

Elsie suddenly brightened. "Oh! But… You *did* come here once – though I suppose you don't remember… It was a *quick* trip… Just between boats… I think I have a picture here somewhere…"

She got up, walked over to a sideboard in the dining room, and pulled open a drawer. "I think it's in this picture book…" Elsie muttered as she pulled out an old photo album and carried it back to the table, flipping through pages as she walked. "Let me see… You were just a little bit of a thing… Yes! Here it is!"

Elsie sat back down and put the album on the table,

A. Gardner Strong

turning it so David could see. She pointed to a black and white photo showing a young Claire holding a baby, and a young boy was sitting on a chair in front of her. "It was the only time your mother came back here since…"

David's mind raced as he scrutinized the photo. "I've seen this picture!" he declared.

"Could be…" Elsie said, pausing to think. "We made two pictures, as I recall, and sent one to Claire…" She pointed to the baby in the picture. "That's you…"

David was rocked back with surprise. "*I'm* the baby? Really?"

Elsie smiled and nodded her head. "I took the picture…" she said with pride.

"Wow…" David's brow wrinkled as he studied the photo, reaching back into his more recent memory. "I found this picture after Mom died! We were sure it was Mother and we figured Amie – my sister – was the baby and that it was me sitting there, but nobody knew where it was taken…"

"You were no more than a month old," Elsie responded gently, a maternal smile on her face. "That's Douglas sitting there…" Her smile faded, replaced by a soft veil of sadness.

"So, that's him…" David mussed. "And this must have been taken in front of the old farmhouse?"

"Yes… It was a long time ago…" Elsie answered sadly.

David paused reflectively. "Can I look at it?"

Elsie straightened her back and pulled the photo album closer in a somewhat protective gesture. "Well... It's just a bunch of old photos... Really nothing you would recognize..."

David shook his head. "No... Not the album! I mean the house! Can I look at the old farmhouse?"

"Oh! Well... I guess that's O.K..." Elsie said with some uncertainty. She got up and walked into the kitchen, carrying the photo album with her. "Let me see..." she pondered as she walked back toward the buttry. "I think Sam keeps a key over here..."

Seventeen

David drove down the hill in his little car, carefully navigating the ancient gravel drive. He parked on the grass, next to the 1830 farmhouse, and got out of the car, reaching back into the rear seat to pull out the rolled up architectural plans he had found in the guest house, back in Westport.

Taking a few steps to the North, toward the water, he stopped at the crest of the rise that separated the house from the narrow roadway. David stood quietly and looked around, gazing for a few minutes at the glistening waters of Upper Pulpit Harbor, stretching past cliffs that protruded out from the near shoreline, dense with evergreen trees. His eyes scanned the opposite shore, moving slowly across the field, then along the dirt driveway, settling on the lovely farmhouse and barn structures across the way at Sunnyside.

He tried to visualize his mother in this setting, but the image wouldn't come. David could see why she would be taken by such a place, but he just couldn't conjure up a mirage of her, say, walking across that dam, for example. Maybe it was because she had been so much younger when she had apparently moved about so freely on this island, and, while he had certainly seen old photos of her, he couldn't really picture her as a young girl; not just yet, anyway.

It was beautiful; simple and serene. Why had she never brought them here? One time as a baby hardly counted. Knowing his parents as he did, it didn't seem to David as though his father would have put up much, if any, resistance if she had ever wanted to shorten their time on Block Island, or even skip it altogether now and again, in favor of this place. A trip to the island would have been a nice change...

David sighed, then turned and looked at the run-down farmhouse owned by his mother. He walked slowly around to the South side and up to the antique front door. Looking at the modern key in his hand, he realized immediately that it wouldn't open this door since the keyhole was clearly designed for a skeleton key. He smiled and moved along to the door in the kitchen ell, which he could see had a more modern bolt type lock. The lock was a little stiff, but after fumbling with the key a bit, the old wooden door swung open.

David slowly walked into the barren house, shocked by how far back in time this abode had apparently stopped being updated. The wallpapers and flooring were well beyond anything he had ever seen, so he was hard pressed to guess if he was looking at 1920 décor or something even older. To begin with, there was an ancient looking hot water tank, an old, discolored, free standing shower unit, and an antique iron sink, all stuffed into the cramped mudroom. In the kitchen, the wallpaper was old and faded, with bright patches clearly marking the spots where pictures, notes, or calendars obviously used to hang. Water stains decorated the corners of the room, as well as the wallpaper immediately surrounding the casements of some of the windows. The wood floor was covered by aging sheets of linoleum, worn bare in spots. An old, white, wood-burning cook stove, with an oven temperature gauge showing the indications "Warm", "Moderate", and "Hot" instead of degrees, served as the centerpiece of the room, sitting proudly beneath a simple mantle, on which David had been instructed to place the key.

The dining room had similarly outdated wallpaper, and the simple ceiling chandelier was discolored and quite dusty. An antique oil fired space heater was hooked up to the central chimney, and while he assumed it was self contained, David saw no buttons or gauges that made sense to him. The living room was a continuation of the same, though the linoleum floor coverings were extremely worn, revealing more of the ancient wood floors, as well as clear signs of some deterioration of the structure.

The center hallway, framed out squarely from the antique front door, with transoms above the doorways to either side, had offered up the biggest surprise when David opened the front hall closet door, also framed neatly below an open transom, only to find it was a water closet. He had jiggled the flush on the toilet, but it was clear that the water had been turned off, probably long ago.

David looked at his watch. He had not been able to get a reservation, so he knew he had to make it back to the ferry terminal down at the village in time to get in line to catch the boat.

He walked back through the house and exited the way he had come in, but he left the old homestead with surprising reluctance. His mother had, for some reason, resolved to restore this crumbling edifice and, according to the architectural plans, she had clearly intended to come back here, after all these years, with her two children. It was difficult, he found, to leave this strange home with it's even stranger connection to his mother's life.

He got back into the car and slowly drove down the old dirt driveway. Up the hill, Elsie sat patiently by the back door window, looking intently down the hill, following David's movements as he drove off, wondering if it would be for the last time.

Eighteen

December 6, 2006

David walked through the main lobby of the hospital without bothering to stop at the information desk, took the elevator up to the fourth floor, and walked down the busy corridor, directly to Room 402, stopping short as he was about to walk through the door. Where Douglas Brown had been lying comatose about a week ago, the bed now held a small, frail, sleeping child, hooked up to various tubes and monitors, just like his predecessor. David stepped back to take a second look at the room placard, thinking he must have gotten off at the wrong floor, but "402" was engraved on it, just as he thought.

He walked back to the nurses' station, his thoughts churning. What had happened to Doug Brown? "Excuse me…" David said, clearing his throat as an afterthought, trying to get the nurse's attention. "Where did you move the patient who was in Room 402?"

"Patient's name?" queried the nurse, looking up at him, clearly annoyed by the interruption.

"Brown… Douglas Brown…" David replied, careful to speak clearly.

"Your relationship?" the nurse asked, her tone flat.

David's mind was buzzing so he missed the question. "I'm sorry?" he asked.

"Your relationship to Mr. Brown?" the nurse pressed.

David shook his head, thinking for a fleeting moment about his argument with Anne. "I'm not related..." he confessed honestly.

"I'm sorry," the nurse responded in an unsympathetic manner, "but I can't give out any information about Mr. Brown."

"Did he die?" David pressed urgently.

The nurse looked over the top of her glasses and softened her tone. "I'm really sorry; Patient confidentiality, you know..."

~

Chief Macomber let out a deep breath. "The parents asked if they could move him closer, and, frankly, I couldn't think of any good reason to say 'No'."

David was obviously relieved that Doug Brown was still alive, but he was still keenly frustrated by his change in venue. "But, shouldn't you be the first one to talk with him when he wakes up?" he asked.

"The instructions are that I am to be called as soon as he regains consciousness, yes," Chief Macomber assured David, "but quite frankly, son, I don't expect to be getting that call".

David's frustration kicked up a notch. "So, what happens to the investigation? How will we know..."

"Listen," Chief Macomber wanted to pick his words carefully, "I understand that you'd like some justice for your mother, David, but, as I told you the other day, I can not file charges against an unconscious man, and I certainly can't do anything if he doesn't make it, you understand?"

"No…" David answered without hesitation.

"If he doesn't pull through," the chief clarified gently, "we will have to close the investigation, rule it an accident, with speed and a potential of mechanical failure being factors, and that's about all we can do."

"Isn't there some way to rule out mechanical failure?" David asked in complete exasperation. "What about the examination and analysis of the wreckage?"

Chief Macomber shook his head. "No… Other than his testimony, we can't really rule it out for sure. There was too much physical damage to the vehicle, and it was a classic car, so there was no computer or black box device…" He felt bad for the kid, but he really wished he could just let it go. "I'm sorry," he continued, genuinely sympathetic in his demeanor. "Like I told you the other day, there was no alcohol or other substance involved, so at this point we know just about everything we could know except why the darn fool was driving so fast…" He shook his head again sadly, sighing deeply as he looked at David's face. This kid was not letting go, he could tell, noting his obvious struggle to keep his emotions in check as he tried to figure out what else he could do.

Nineteen

December 7, 2006

 riday had seemed endless for both David and Peter, for different reasons, but they were both extremely happy to greet the end of the week. They were seated comfortably at the dining room table, at a ninety degree angle to one another, enjoying a delicious meal, prepared and served by Alice. They had each just consumed a large bowl of chunky lobster bisque, and now a lovely dinner plate of boneless stuffed chicken breast, corn, and crispy fried sweet potatoes was being served.

David looked at Alice appreciatively. "Thank you!" he said warmly.

"Yes, thank you, Alice!" Peter echoed. "That was delicious! Much better than anything I've had in New York lately."

Alice smiled. "You're just saying that, Mr. Winslow…" she demurred.

"I mean every word!" Peter responded with great sincerity.

Alice smiled as she carried off the soup bowls, followed by Jack, tail wagging, alert for any treats that might come his way. David's smile faded and he cleared his throat. "So, how *was* New York, Dad?"

"Fine, I guess…" Peter shrugged. "It was O.K.…."

"So, what did you do?" David asked, feeling there was a good deal more on his father's mind.

Peter thought for a moment. "I don't know… I kept myself busy…" He looked at his plate, then back at David. "It's all pretty much a blur, to be honest; Very strange…"

"What do you mean?" David pressed.

"Well…" Peter shook his head. "People were funny…" he observed softly, shrugging as if to emphasize the degree to which he found this experience perplexing. "Everyone was fussing about — *very* polite — but deliberately still saying *nothing* personal; Afraid they'll upset me, I guess…" He took a deep breath and let it out with a sigh. "I don't know…" he repeated, shaking his head. "Talk about avoiding the pink elephant in the room!" Peter was more than ready to change the discussion. "So, how about you? What did you do while I was gone?"

"Nothing much, really…" David answered cautiously. "I did drive back up to Maine…"

Peter looked surprised. "To the island? Was that wise? I really hate to see you spinning your wheels…"

"I just thought it would help me figure out…"

Peter shook his head. "I hope you didn't bother the Browns…"

David took a forkful of food and chewed for a moment. "I just talked a little with Mrs. Brown…"

"You really shouldn't worry those people, David…" Peter admonished gently. "I *know* how you feel, but Doug is still in a coma; I'm sure his parents have enough on their plates…" He paused for a moment. "Please keep in mind that your mother was very protective of them…"

"I know, Dad…"

"Things will get better…"

Peter worked at his food in silence; David looked at his food without eating. "Dad…" he ventured. "Did you know Mother owns their home up there?"

Peter looked up. "On the island? Well…" He thought for a moment. "I think they had some problem with taxes a few years back… I'm sure it has to do with that. You know how your mother sometimes got carried away by her passion for 'fixing' things…" Peter hesitated, took a forkful of food, and chewed slowly, thoughtfully. He looked down when tears started to creep into his eyes. David regarded him with real love and compassion, knowing how hard it must be for him to think about his great loss.

Peter shook his head slightly and continued. "If she put the property in her name to help them, I think we should just sign it back over to the Browns. I'm sure that's what she would want…"

David leaned back in his chair. "I agree, Dad, but," he hesitated and then continued, "actually, Mom split the property and built – had *Doug* build — a new house for the Browns," he paused for a moment, "but I think she planned to restore the old farmhouse for us – for Amie and me. I... I found the plans in the guest house."

Peter looked surprised but thoughtful. "Hmmm... I suppose that makes sense..." He reflected for a moment. "I keep thinking about all the little things she talked about in the last few months... I... I think she was feeling some nostalgia lately... She *did* say something, months ago, about it being sad that you and your sister didn't know her island..."

David leaned back in toward his father. "Did Mom ever really *talk* with you about the island?"

"No..." Peter responded slowly. "Not that much... She did a lot to help those people, but it was never really something we discussed a great deal. You know..." he paused for a moment, "whatever your mother did with her money, I never had any issue with it." He looked at David, wanting to be sure he understood. "I mean, her mother left her a small fortune, and she was always doing things to help other people – *especially* on that island..." He blinked quickly, fighting back a sudden urge to weep. "Your mother was a good person..." Peter summarized softly. He took a sip of water and sat quietly for a minute.

David, likewise, took a sip of water and shifted back in his chair before breaking the silence. "Dad... Dad, I've thought a lot about this; I think I'd like to finish what she started".

Peter looked startled. "What do you mean?"

"Well, I thought I could stay up there – on the island – for a while..." David responded carefully. "It's like – I feel *connected* to Mom up there – in some *strange* way. I mean," he paused for a moment, "there are people up there who *knew* Mom..." He paused to let the words sink in, as much as to formulate his next words. "I think it would help me come to terms with some of this..."

Peter leaned forward. "But, what would you do?"

"Well, I thought I could organize and oversee the work she had planned to do..."

Peter considered this seriously for a moment. "But, if she planned this as a project for Doug to do, I'm pretty sure she did that as part of her vision of how she would take care of the Brown family."

David shrugged his shoulders. "Well, that may be true, but I think she really *wanted* to do this..." he said, almost pleadingly to his father. "*He's* not in a position to do anything, Dad," he continued. "I think Mom would want the work done – one way or another, and I'm sure I can find some other contractors to do the work."

"I don't know..." Peter mused warily.

David took a deep breath and looked earnestly at his father. "I really want to do this, Dad," he pressed. "I want to do it for Mom..."

Twenty

December 8, 2006

The drive along Maine's coastal route can be quite interesting and varied, shifting from fast-paced sterile highways to narrow, winding two-lane country roads with little transition or warning, meandering along through quaint New England towns, isolated farm lands, and overdeveloped stretches with scattered shops and strip malls, sporadically revealing dramatic views of the frigid waters along the approximately 3,478 miles of tidally-influenced coastline.

This time was different for David, the third time truly being the charm for him. Instead of driving with a single minded determination to get there, David took his time and really looked around at the scenery as he traveled North, headed for the Mid Coast region.

He braked to slow to the 25 MPH limit, going down the gently curving hill in Wiscasset, the self described "Prettiest Village" of Maine, and as he slowly rolled down the sloping grade he observed charming antique shops, banks, an inn, and restaurants, all located in beautifully constructed and maintained Victorian and Colonial style structures. Finally approaching the long, fairly modern bridge that spanned the Sheepscot River, David spotted Red's off to the left, and made a mental note to come back through Wiscasset when outdoor seating was in season. He had read that Red's served up the best lobster sandwich in the country and, looking at the tiny shack and stacked plastic chairs on the deck, David had a gut feeling that the reviews were probably right on target.

As he continued his long drive up US Route 1, David wondered often at the beauty of the countryside, was taken aback by the pockets of poverty, and was thrilled, at times, to see the ocean splashing on the rocks along the rugged coastline. He would be back in Summer, he knew; He would explore this "foreign" territory more carefully.

Finally, the fenced quarry and cement plant in Thomaston gave way to the infinitely more charming downtown and waterfront area in Rockland. David stopped at the ferry terminal to use the bathroom and to buy his ticket, happy to find out that he could get a reservation for the 5:15 p.m. boat. He wouldn't have to wait in line this time. He had forty-five minutes to spare before he had to be back to present his ticket to the security officer. He turned out of the parking lot and continued North on Route 1, past the commercial buildings and strip malls and into Rockport, where he started seeing signs for the Penobscot Bay Medical Center.

He took the right at the traffic light and drove down the long drive, past the medical building, into the visitor parking lot. As he walked to the front entrance he was struck by the beauty of the setting, overlooking Penobscot Bay. "Quite an improvement over the noisy congestion of Providence…" he thought.

Once inside, he quickly located the Information Desk and in less than a minute he was walking away holding in his hand a scrap of paper with a room number written on it.

Walking through a set of double doors, he passed a somber looking young woman and her teenage daughter, he assumed, apparently leaving the hospital. David paused and looked back at them for a minute, watching them disappear down the corridor. Something was familiar about these two people. Maybe it was something about the woman's red hair? He felt as though he had definitely seen at least one of them before, but he could not quite make the connection. He had a boat to catch, however, and didn't have time to waste, so he turned around and pressed on.

After a few minutes, David entered the room marked "220" where he silently looked in at the comatose Douglas Brown. "Good," he thought with a sense of relief. There was still hope. It was still possible that he could sort out all those agonizing loose ends. With a deep sigh, stemming from something inside that approached satisfaction, David turned and left the hospital, heading back toward the ferry terminal and his rendezvous with destiny.

Twenty-one

Like clockwork, the North Island ferry had arrived on time, unloaded, loaded, and was once again departing Rockland Harbor, moving steadily past the breakwater and light house, into Penobscot Bay.

In spite of the chill and the evening hour, David stood on the deck for about ten minutes, watching thoughtfully as the ferry progressed through the harbor. He finally had to retreat to the warmth and shelter of his car as the ferry approached picturesque Owls Head Light, its brilliant strobe reaching out in the dark.

The island experience was starting to feel, oddly enough, like a relationship that had passed the threshold of dating and was now moving headlong into a state of lifelong commitment. David was now eager to absorb all the beauty and subtle nuances of his new bride.

The sky was fully dark by the time the ferry pulled into the North Island dock, the crew well prepared to unload the passengers quickly so they could secure the vessel and get home for supper. In the course of the hour and ten minutes since leaving Rockland, David's spirits had risen for the first time since having received news of the accident. This part *was* for his mother. It was not fair to say that he had transcended the pain of having been forever denied a satisfactory final encounter with her, but he was filled with a sense that he was truly in the process of assimilating a critical segment of his mother's life, and his spirits were lifted up beyond his expectations.

As he waited his turn to drive off the ferry, David never noticed the white truck, parked further back on the deck, between the cabins. He was focused now on reclaiming his mother's island, and could hardly wait to shift his car into second gear knowing that, for the first time, he would be driving through the parking lot, taking a right at Main Street, and continuing on to his own place to live, at least for the time being...

~

A hard dose of reality awaited him, however, as he approached the Circa 1830 Farmhouse, a spring in his step and a flashlight in his hand. Elsie had left the key under an old plant pot, as promised, and the electricity had been turned back on, also as expected, but upon entering the house, with darkness all around outside, David found it was cold and dreary.

Walking through the dimly lit kitchen, past the dining room, and into the middle bedroom, David dropped his bedroll, knapsack, and tool kit on the floor. He hadn't really thought through the part about arriving in the dark and cold of night, but his determination wasn't going to desert him at these small bumps in the road. He looked around for a minute and then opened the tool kit and fished out a screwdriver and plumbing wrench, then pulled a new copy of "The Idiot's guide to Plumbing" out of his bag, and walked back into the dining room.

David first looked over the old oil fired space heater in the dining room, for just a moment or two, but quickly ruled out messing around with it at that point. He proceeded back into the kitchen, put down the book and tools, and scrutinized the old wood cook stove. He had never seen one like this, but he had plenty of experience with the fireplaces in Westport and the Vermont Castings stove on Block Island, so he felt confident that he could get it going, in spite of the fact that it had been sitting idle for some time.

He found some kindling materials behind the stove. The wood box wasn't full, but he calculated that there was enough wood to last for several days if he was careful; enough to get him started. He quickly figured out the damper set up, then, looking on the mantle, found an old box of safety matches, with just a few matches left inside. He took out a match and lit the stove, smiling as the flame caught on quickly. He could smell dust burning as the stove heated up, but that would pass, he knew.

Plumbing. Elsie had mentioned, when pressed, that the well pump in the basement hadn't been on for a while. David located the basement door – thankful that there actually was one in a house this old – and switched on his flashlight again before descending the somewhat rustic flight of stairs.

The basement, he found, was not especially welcoming either. The dirt floor offered up a rich, earthen aroma, unknown to those who have always lived in homes of modern construction. David quickly adjusted his eyes in the dim light and looked over various ancient pipes and connections until he thought he had figured out what needed to be turned on to get water into the house. He was relieved when the well pump kicked on, but he quickly noticed a few suspicious drips in the visible plumbing.

David raced upstairs again, realizing that he needed to use the toilet. He pulled the chain on the overhead light in the water closet and bent down to look around the aging porcelain fixture, trying to find the water shutoff. He found only straight pipes coming out of the floor.

David pressed the flush on the toilet, but nothing happened. Frustrated, but determined, he stood up and lifted the cover off the tank, only to find that it was bone dry. He closed his eyes for a moment trying to remember the plumbing configuration he had just been looking at in the basement, wondering if he would be increasing his list of problems if he were to use the toilet without water.

He couldn't be sure. Suddenly he remembered looking at the freestanding woodshed when he was here last time, when it was still daylight, and thinking that there might be an old out-house attached to it.

David made haste to go outside, flashlight again in hand, to test his theory, hoping desperately to find some "original" provisions for nature, in keeping with the wallpaper and woodwork. Failing that, he was prepared to settle for a discrete clump of bushes, if need be, rather than risk the plumbing in the house. His hunch was soon rewarded. When he opened the door to the smaller shed attached to the wood shed, the beam of his flashlight revealed that it was, indeed, an old fashioned out house with a classic two-seater arrangement.

He exhaled softly and stepped in. It would do for the moment...

Twenty-two

December 9, 2006

The little Islander store was surprisingly like the IGA David had seen near T.F. Greene Airport in Rhode Island. He had been killing time once, waiting for Anne to arrive on a SouthWest flight from Florida, and had noticed the little store only because the name was "Dave's Market". He had parked and gone in out of idle curiosity, but had walked out with a nice, hot cup of coffee and a massive chocolate chip cookie. Like the IGA, the Islander had neat rows of dry and canned foods, condiments, and baking ingredients, paper goods, and refrigerated cabinets, filled with fresh and frozen food. David wandered around, assessing the somewhat limited options, as he picked up a box of safety matches and two jars of baked beans.

He walked back past the check out and stopped in front of the store bulletin board that he had noticed coming in. It was covered with a variety of business cards and hand printed notices, attached in a reasonably organized fashion by colorful push pins. David fished a small spiral notebook out of his pocket and started writing down names of plumbers, "land improvement" specialists, and building contractors. "It shouldn't be too hard to get some help," he thought with a measure of self satisfaction, assuming that there couldn't possibly be much demand in the off season.

Meanwhile, the cashier, who had been turned away from the check-out counter when David passed by, was now talking on the phone. "…I don't know…" David could hear her clearly say. "They won't tell me anything because we're divorced... No... they won't tell her anything because she's a minor... No... You know Elsie..."

Hearing Elsie's name, David started to really pay attention. He put the notebook back in his pocket and moved over to the check-out counter with his items, waiting for the cashier to notice him.

David studied her closely now and recalled seeing this mass of red hair before. She glanced over her shoulder, taking notice of David, but just lowered her voice and continued on with her phone conversation without acknowledging him directly. "Well, you know how she is... Hey... I got a customer... O.K.... Bye..."

The cashier hung up the phone and stepped over to the cash register. She was not smiling but was polite. She quickly rang up David's items. "That will be $4.59, please."

"Oh..." David started to say something about seeing her before as he pulled out his money, but he paused and asked instead, "How much is a cup of coffee?"

"Small, medium, or large?" came the impersonal reply.

"Um... medium."

"$1.50. Do you want one?"

"Yes... Please."

"$6.17 then..."

David was surprised by the automaton-like demeanor. In a community where drivers waved a greeting to every passing car and pedestrian, her flat communication seemed totally out of place. "Here you go..." he said with a smile, handing her the money and waiting for change.

"You help yourself to the coffee... Over there..." she said, pointing to the counter where the coffee urns and coffee cups were set up.

"Oh... O.K., thanks...." David smiled again then paused, looking at the cashier for a moment. "I'm sorry, but have we met before?" he asked, taking the proverbial bull by the horns.

The cashier considered this, if only for a moment. "No, I don't believe so..."

David blushed slightly. "Sorry... You just look familiar..."

The cashier looked at his face without smiling, and with no telltale flirting or pleasure in her demeanor. "Well, who *are* you?"

"Oh, of course... David... David Winslow..."

A startled look crept into her eyes. "You're from Boston?"

"Well, not exactly..." David countered, though he often identified himself as being from Boston, just to narrow down the geographic region. "Westport... Massachusetts," he added quickly, knowing most people seemed to only know of Westport, Connecticut, thanks, in part, to Martha Stewart.

"You must be related to Claire Winslow?" the cashier ventured, narrowing her eyes.

"She was my mother…"

"Oh…"

David poured his coffee and broke the awkward silence. "Did you know her?"

"No…"

"Oh… Well… I'm trying to sort out the old farmhouse she owned…"

The cashier took a step backward as if to distance herself. "The old Winthrop place?"

David looked momentarily puzzled. "Well, I guess it was the Brown place…"

The cashier looked off out the front windows of the little store. "It was the caretaker's house… They were just the caretakers for the Winthrop place…" she responded, a trace of something like bitterness detectable in her voice.

"Sunnyside?" David asked, trying to further the conversation.

"Yes…" she answered, her attention suddenly focusing on the shelves. "I'm sorry… I have to stock the shelves…" she murmured as she reached over and took the key out of the register and started to walk away.

David was a bit surprised by the abrupt turn in the conversation, but he was immediately apologetic. "Oh…

Of course!" he conceded. "I didn't mean to keep you from your work; I'm sorry…"

The cashier paused and looked directly at David, her eyes distant, but sad. "I'm sorry about your mother…" she said before walking away.

"Thanks…" David replied, wondering more than ever what her story was.

~

Elsie was just finishing up washing the breakfast dishes when the door bell rang. She wiped her hands on a cloth kitchen towel and walked over to open the front door. She took the precaution of peeking out the window first, then she opened the door wide.

"David…" she greeted her visitor with a warm smile.

"Hi!" David answered with a lingering smile.

"Is there something I can help you with?" she asked, not inviting him in.

"No…" David responded, shaking his head. "I just wanted to thank you for leaving the key out for me."

Elsie smiled again. "You're welcome," she replied. "Just let me know if you need anything else."

"Well… Thanks again…" David said and turned to go then, stopped and turned back quickly, reaching out to prevent the door from closing in his face. "Oh, I'm sorry! I did want to ask you something," he said, then added, "May I?" as he stepped forward and over the threshold, into the foyer. Elsie took a few steps back and allowed David to close the door behind him. It was chilly out, after all. As he moved forward, David continued talking. "Will you and Mr. Brown be getting over to see your son now that he's here in Rockland?"

Elsie hesitated, her discomfort evident through her smile. "Oh... I'll be going over when I can get a ride," she responded softly, her guard obviously up. "It's too expensive to take a taxi there from the ferry."

"Well..." David smiled, trying to put her at ease. "I'll be back and forth... picking up supplies or whatever. I'd be happy to drive you sometime..."

"Oh... Well..." Elsie groped for a response, clearly taken off guard by the offer. "I'm sure I'll get a ride from the outreach worker, or one of the ladies at church... But thanks..."

David, still smiling, nodded his head and started to turn, reaching out to open the door, but he hesitated and turned back again. Elsie had turned away to head to the kitchen. "Oh! You know..." he said, stopping Elsie in her tracks. "Maybe you can tell me something? Who is the cashier down at the little Islander store?"

Elsie hesitated for a moment but slowly continued walking back to the kitchen. "Oh... Which one?" she asked, innocence dripping from her voice. "There are several girls, you know, taking turns down there..."

"Well, she's a bit on the tall side..." David offered, wondering if, in fact, there were several different cashiers employed by this tiny store. "Red hair..."

Elsie reached the kitchen and stopped by the sink, turning to look over toward David, still standing by the door. "Sounds like Angie..." she said after a moment's hesitation. "She's Ed Cooper's youngest daughter..." She looked at David. "Any reason in particular?"

"Oh... Just curious..." David answered with a shrug. "She looked a little familiar..."

"Well..." Elsie suggested, forcing a smile, "you probably saw her downtown or at the ferry when you were here last time."

"You're probably right..." David agreed, satisfied for the moment that he at least had a name to attach to the familiar stranger. "Well, have a good day..." His smile faded as he turned away, opened the door, walked out without further ado, and closed the door behind him.

Elsie stood at the kitchen sink, a troubled expression on her face. She looked furtively out the window, tracking David as he walked down the hill toward the old farmhouse. "Well," she thought, "there's no way he's going to survive the hardships of that old house for very long..."

But a piece of her was not quite so sure.

Twenty-three

December 10, 2006

Having been entirely focused on getting the heat and plumbing sorted out, David had located the stair case to the second floor, but had not taken the time to go up there to look around, partly because he knew, given the lack of central heating, that it was bound to be on the uncomfortable side of cold. Visiting the attic for the first time, he was pleasantly surprised to find an antique bed frame and a few small tables in the large open area, and an entire bedroom set in one of the four small bedrooms that surrounded the perimeter of the loft space. Judging by the thick carpet of dust, David felt certain there had been no human intervention in this area for decades. Obviously these had not been among the items Elsie had deemed necessary to take with her up to the new house, but it was surprising, nonetheless, to find this treasure-trove left behind, almost as if the previous occupants had all simply let it slip their collective minds.

David toyed with the idea of bringing the bedroom set down to the middle bedroom, closest to the space heater, but in the end, he was more intrigued by the antique bed frame. He could have a mattress set brought over from Rockland, he was certain. He would ask Elsie about the history of this bed, but as he carefully stripped back the thick gray mass that had naturally encapsulated the delicately hand painted headboard, he was certain his decision would meet his mother's approval.

~

The sun rose the next day against a wall of thick ground fog, wrapping the old farmhouse in a delicate shroud. If one were to have looked about at just the right moment, they would have seen the old elm at the East end of the drive lit up with a halo-like effect as the trajectory of the sun brought it perfectly in line with the abundant crown of the aging tree.

By the time David boarded the ferry, the fog had lifted, revealing another beautiful but chilly morning. As the North Island ferry advanced past the breakwater light house, headed toward the docks in Rockland, the day had warmed somewhat and David felt lifted by the potential accomplishments of his first official day-trip to the mainland.

~

The little sleep shop, just a block or so beyond the Brown Bag, wasn't open when he first arrived, so David pressed on to the next stop on his list. Continuing North, he easily found the Home Depot, sitting high atop a hill, looming large above Route 1.

David parked his car, grabbed a shopping cart, and quickly zeroed in on the plumbing section. He had never been in a Home Depot before, much less purchased plumbing supplies, so he was quickly overwhelmed by what seemed like a vast assortment of toilet brands and models. To his great relief, a plumbing clerk, identified by his orange apron and name badge, came to his rescue before long, and soon he was standing in the check-out line, his oversized cart loaded with a new toilet bowl, tank, seat, and various other plumbing supplies that had been pressed on him by his helpful assistant.

~

David turned left out of the Home Depot parking lot and continued North, finding the regional medical complex for the second time without any difficulty. He turned right on Hospital Drive and followed it past the medical building, pulling into the Pen Bay Medical Center visitor parking lot. Trying to be forward thinking, as was his norm, he carefully parked in an end spot, away from the heavy traffic, making it easier to maneuver out of the space, given that his little car was now bulging with his Home Depot purchases. It had not been easy, stuffing the equivalent of a small truck load into his little two seater, but with a little ingenuity and a fully reclining passenger seat, he managed to get it all in. He felt he had done well so far, and looked very certain and calm as he walked across the visitor's parking lot and into the front lobby.

~

Once inside, David walked past the reception desk and proceeded directly to Room 220. He didn't enter the room, but stood quietly in the doorway for several minutes, looking intently at Douglas Brown as he continued to lay there in a coma. No change, but he was still alive. There was hope...

~

By 1:30 p.m., David had stopped at the sleep store to buy a mattress set and arrange delivery, and was back at the ferry terminal in Rockland, sitting in his car, waiting for the 2:15 boat, a sandwich and cup of coffee from the Brown Bag serving as his lunch. He had a reservation so he did not have to be there so early, but it was pointless for him to try and go anywhere else, David reasoned, since the car was already overstuffed with plumbing supplies.

Arranging for delivery of the bedding had been a good deal more complicated and expensive than he had anticipated, but David now had a greater appreciation as to why so many islanders had pick-up trucks! The idea of living on an island seemed like a glorious freedom to the innocent mainlander, but it was, David was quickly learning, considerably more costly and very much constrained by the limitations of the ferry schedule.

At about 1:40 p.m., the ferry from North Island pulled up to the dock, and cars, trucks, and walking passengers quickly unloaded. Although David wasn't really paying close attention, his eyes were suddenly drawn to a white truck being driven by Angela Cooper. There was someone else in the cab, but he could not make out who the passenger was. David opened his window for a better look, but the truck had quickly driven off the ramp and straight up the hill to Main Street. David watched it as it turned right, just as a ferry agent approached his open window, hand outreached, demanding "Ticket please?"

David handed the agent his ticket, then looked back over his shoulder where the truck had just disappeared around the corner. The agent smiled and motioned toward the loading ramp. "You're all set," he announced. "You can just drive right on down."

David smiled back. "Thanks..." He shifted the car into gear and pulled forward, instinctively looking back over his shoulder again as he pulled out of the reservation line.

~

The sun was still shining brightly when David pulled up to the side of the old farmhouse and got out. He started immediately removing the newly purchased plumbing materials from the little car, glad to be able to quickly restore it's sense of sporty dignity. He pulled the new toilet bowl out of the car and set it on the grass, next to the house, then he went back and took out the somewhat lighter toilet tank and carried it directly into the house.

~

David had been disappointed that neither island plumber had returned his calls, but he was determined to get the basics under control. He had his plumbing guide; He was sure he could figure it out.

After a lot of prep work, David carefully threaded a new shower head onto the existing copper plumbing and then stood back, with great satisfaction, to admire his handiwork. He quickly got back to work and looked around to the back of the shower stall, then reached down to turn on the water at the base. He reached inside the stall and set the knob to the three-quarter mark, but was disappointed and perplexed when nothing happened.

~

Back outside, dusk was closing in as David carefully gathered the remaining plumbing materials in his arms and shut the car door. Starting back to the house, he was momentarily startled, thinking he had heard something. "Hello?" he asked tentatively, but got no reply. He turned his head, looking and listening. After a minute he resumed the immediate task at hand, lugging the rest of his purchases into the house, with the exception of the new toilet bowl. He would deal with that later; Even better, maybe an actual plumber would deal with it! It would be fine sitting there, for now. He paused once more, thinking that he saw a rustling in a nearby evergreen, but he did not see the cause, so he continued back to the house.

~

Aside from the time at the hospital, David realized, as he later heated up some baked beans on the kitchen stove, his thoughts had not been dwelling on his mother's death and Doug's life all day, and he was intrigued by the way this realization made him feel. On the one hand, he felt a sharp pang of guilt; Survivor's guilt, perhaps? He quickly pushed that feeling aside, knowing it was unwarranted.

He remembered the time his Keeshond died when the dog had followed him across the street to retrieve a ball, and a car had come out of nowhere. He thought about the way his mother had helped him through that traumatic period of sorrow and guilt. She had gently gathered up the lifeless body of his faithful friend, carefully wrapping her in one of her best sheets, and carried her into the front garden, cradled in her left arm so she could hold her son's hand tightly with her right hand. The ceremony had been private and tearful, just the two of them, and David was certain that his mother's tears had been at least ninety percent born of relief that it was the dog she was burying, not her son. After she had set a rugged stone on top of the new mound, and replanted the flowers she had disturbed around this new monument, she had held him tightly, dried off his tears, then bundled him into her car and swooped him off to the matinee showing of "The Neverending

Story". Her arm wrapped tightly around him, they had sat in the darkened and, thankfully, nearly empty theater, tears rolling down his cheeks. But slowly, the story had drawn him in, and he remembered leaving the theater feeling a little distance between himself and the morning tragedy. It had taken some time for him to assimilate the sorrow and guilt, but his mother had wisely given him a brief "vacation" from his overwhelming grief, and that had helped to give him perspective.

The farmhouse, the heating and plumbing problems, the challenge of transporting normal household goods to the island, all these things had become his own Neverending Story, and he felt his mother's arm around him for the first time in weeks.

Twenty-four

December 11, 2006

Sunrise came the next morning, once again through a thick, low lying fog, the red/orange ball of the sun, looming large in the East, swathed in a delicate translucent gauze. David closed the front door and trotted quickly to the out house. The base of the new toilet was still sitting on the grass next to the house, obscured only slightly by the ethereal mist in the air.

~

David finished his newly acquired rustic morning routine and hopped into his car, turning out quickly and heading down the long drive, his whole being craving a healthy dose of caffeine. He was soon standing at the counter of the Islander, holding a package of toilet paper and a large cup of freshly brewed coffee. The cashier was an older woman with a ready smile, someone David had not seen before. "see ya later, Freda..." said a burly fisherman as he left the store with his steaming cup of coffee and half eaten pastry in hand.

"See ya..." Freda turned her smile on David. "That it, young man?"

"Yes, thanks..." David answered with a smile. "For now, anyway."

"O.k., then... That'll be $3.99" Freda calculated smartly, eying the stranger before her as if she were divining tea leaves.

David handed her a five dollar bill. "Say..." he ventured boldly, "you know the young woman who was working here yesterday, just about this time? When will she be here again?"

Freda raised her eyebrows and cocked her head, as if considering the question. Noting her hesitation, David smiled and tried to aid his cause. "I just wanted to speak to her about something we talked about yesterday," he explained in a confidential tone. "I need a little help with something..."

Freda continued to scrutinize David, but appeared to accept his explanation. "Well, Angie's usually here to open up for me," she replied, "but with her husband in the hospital," she elaborated, "I expect that her schedule will be a bit erratic." She paused and squinted her eyes. "I expect she'll be in this time tomorrow morning," she continued, then quickly added, "Is there anything I can help you with?"

David absorbed this new information. "Well, actually... Can you recommend a good plumber? I've called everyone on your board here, but nobody's called me back yet..."

The phone rang sharply just then and Freda turned away to answer it quickly, not wanting the jarring sound to have a second chance to rattle her nerves. "Islander... No, sorry... She's over there in Rockland with Olivia to check in on Dougie... No... Not really... Listen, I've got some customers... I'll tell her you called... O.K.... Bye now..."

David quickly processed this additional information before Freda hung up the phone and had his face composed in a smile by the time she had turned back to face him. Giving him a hard look, Freda stretched and stifled a yawn, then reached up and rubbed the back of her neck as if in deep thought before addressing David again. "A plumber you say? Well, I don't rightly know... Everyone's kind of *busy* these days..."

~

David was about to go directly back to the old farmhouse, but, at the last minute, he abruptly turned right and drove up the hill on the newer gravel driveway, and pulled into the parking space next to the 1941 Chevy pickup.

Inside the barn house, Elsie was taking a sweater out of the front closet when the doorbell rang. She quickly slipped the sweater over her shoulders and turned to open the door. She was surprised to find David standing there, his cup of coffee in his hand, a serious look on his face.

"Good morning!" she said, her automatic smile kicking in, albeit with a slight nervous twitch in the corners of her mouth. She did not get the feeling that he was stopping by to say farewell. Not that she didn't like him; She truly had tender feelings for him because of his mother. She just didn't want him here.

"Good morning..." David replied automatically, then, without preamble, he got right to the reason he had decided to stop by. "I don't understand why you didn't tell me Angela Cooper was really your son's wife?"

Elsie was momentarily stunned, but quickly recovered her wits and, rather than answer David directly, she motioned him in. "Come, sit down..." she murmured.

David submitted to her direction, feeling he had not

been as tactful as he should have been. He walked into the Morning room and sat at the table, waiting patiently as Elsie went into the kitchen to retrieve her cup of tea before sitting opposite him. She played with her tea bag; Her eyes did not meet his when she finally spoke. "I thought it best to keep her out of this," she defended herself, quietly yet clearly resolute in her position. "I don't see how *every* little detail can be so important…"

David shook his head in disbelief. "But it's a *big* detail!" he replied, gently yet firmly. "I mean, you're right: It clearly doesn't tell me what I really want to know, but still… *Why* keep it from me? Why make me think her name is Angie Cooper when it's really Angie Brown?"

Elsie looked at him, not ready to concede. "But… the two of them got divorced several years ago…"

David shrugged. "Fine… But, I asked you *specifically* about her… Why not just be honest with me? How could it *possibly* hurt for me to know they were married?"

"It's *his* dirty laundry…" Elsie said, looking away again.

"'Dirty laundry'?!" David was incredulous. "He has a daughter… Your granddaughter!" A new thought occurred to him. "My mother knew about all this, I assume? …before she had him come down to work in Westport?"

Elsie answered cautiously, clearly on the defensive. "I really don't recall if your mother and I… talked about it…" she replied, shaking her head and looking down, her focus once again on her tea bag. This was not a conversation she wanted to have and she was now desperate to switch the subject. "I have to get the laundry done before Sam comes in looking for his dinner," she announced, pushing back her chair and rising to indicate the interview was at an end. "I expect you have a lot to take care of yourself," she concluded, summoning her dignity along with her best smile. He was raised right, she was certain; He would take the hint.

Twenty-five

David returned to the old farmhouse and, after a quick bowl of cereal, he decided to try his hand at installing the new toilet. Not a single plumber had returned his call, and the out-house, while possessing a certain rustic charm, was certainly wearing thin. At least it was cold so it didn't really smell – but it was cold!

It took the rest of the morning and the better part of the afternoon, but David was happy to finally be fastening the new toilet seat on his newly installed toilet bowl. It was just a little loose, but David blamed that on the slightly irregular floor. He could make it one-hundred percent sturdy later; For now, it worked, so he could overlook the fact that it wasn't perfect! The sweat and grime on his face and hands showed with unmistakable clarity that he had done all the work himself, and he wore it, momentarily, as a badge of honor. He smiled thinking that his mother would be, in equal parts, proud and horrified by what he had done and how he looked at that moment.

~

The daylight was quickly turning to dusk as David finished a two minute shower in his free standing shower stall and dashed back into the kitchen, wrapped in a large bath towel, happy to be able to dry himself by the blazing wood stove. He made a mental note to look at new hot water heaters tomorrow.

A short while later, David sat at his make-shift dining room table, watching the evening news on one of two stations he was able to get on his little television, equipped with a fully extended rabbit-ear antenna. Fortunately he hadn't come here planning to watch a lot of t.v.! He was just about to put a forkful of steaming baked beans into his mouth, when a dull sound caught his attention. He paused, pressing the mute button on the television remote and listening carefully for a moment, but heard nothing more. He was about to put the sound back on and start to eat again when he heard a clear knocking sound.

He put his fork down and got up, walking to the kitchen door first, then quickly backtracked to the front door. He turned on the hall light and opened the door, surprised to see Angela Brown standing there, an apprehensive look on her face.

"Hi!" he greeted her, opening the door wide.

Angela didn't move. "Freda says you were asking about me..."

"Come in..." David offered, gesturing toward the warm dining room.

"No... No, thanks..." Angela shifted uncomfortably. "No point feeding the rumor mill; People 'round here talk quite enough as it is..."

David looked confused. "Why?..."

Angela shrugged. "Look..." she started then paused, looking down at her shoes as if in thought. "You most likely saw me at the hospital..." she continued, lifting her eyes to meet his. She took a breath and David started to say something, but she held up a hand to stop him. "They say you came in after me one day; I should have said something when I met you at the store, but…" She paused again, not sure what to say. "This is all very *hard*… and confusing…"

David looked at her, still confused but with compassion. "I'm sorry…"

"I… I hear you're angry and want to make him pay for what he did to your mother – and I *get* that…" she continued, looking hard at David.

David stood straighter at this statement, his defenses beginning to kick in. "Do you?" he asked, shaken by this surprising assault. "Do you really? I mean… I'm sorry… I'm not angry at *you*…" he said, though his tone did nothing to reassure her. "But… I will *never* see my mother again… *Never*…" He looked at her directly, then tried to soften his tone. "Yes, I… I guess I *am* angry about that… She must have suffered a *horrible* death…" He paused, blinking back sudden tears. "I *am* angry about that…" he continued, shaking his head. "Nothing can *change* it… But I still really *need* to understand *why* this happened…"

Angela looked almost pleadingly at David. "I'm sorry… I can't help you… I have *no* idea why he was driving so fast; It's not like him to do something so reckless. But I just want you to know that going after him *won't* make it better…"

David shifted his stare for a moment to nothing in particular as he drew a deep breath, then looked back at Angela. "I… I understand that punishing him for what he did will not bring my mother back… I really do get that…"

"If he pulls through and you turn around and put him in jail, the only one you'll be punishing is my little girl..." she pressed, her voice almost a whisper.

David shifted uncomfortably looking at the anguish in Angela's face. "It... It's not my intension to hurt anyone..." he assured her, shaking his head. "It isn't really even my choice..."

"Then please just leave it alone..." she said, her eyes clearly pleading in earnest. "I *truly* feel sorry for your loss... Everyone does. Your mother was like a saint to these people..."

"How do I just... let it go?"

"I don't know... I'm sorry... I really am... But my daughter is praying that her Daddy is going to get better and come home, and I hope that can happen..." Angela concluded, looking sadly at David. She drew a deep breath. "I've got to go... Thank you for your time. Please think about what I said..."

She looked at David for a moment, then turned and quickly moved away from the light. David watched as she got into her white truck and backed it into the driveway before pulling out. He was surprised to see the silhouettes of a young girl and a dog clearly sitting in the passenger seat.

Twenty-six

December 12, 2006

The next morning, David put the cover on a large cup of coffee, picked a fresh blueberry muffin out of the case, and moved over to the cash register, handing five dollars to Angela. "Morning..." he said tenuously, not sure what to expect.

Angela nodded in acknowledgement of David's greeting, but she quickly looked away, focusing on the money. She offered the change to David but he dropped it in the TIP cup by the register.

"Thank you..." Angela said in a voice barely above a whisper.

David nodded, looking momentarily at Angela, then he turned and walked out with his coffee and muffin, feeling more than a little awkward, and strangely innocent at the same time. He certainly meant her – or anyone, for that matter – no harm whatsoever. He felt badly, but he knew he was not responsible for creating the problems she had laid at his doorstep.

~

David had taken a right out of the Islander parking lot, heading down to the village, and now stood at the end of the dock, talking on his cell phone. This was, he had discovered, one of the few places that he could get good reception. He hated to do it at this point, but he could see a land line at the old farmhouse in the near future.

He had made several calls to contractors, and now he was trying to get through to his father. "Hey, Dad..."

he said to his father's voice mail. They had swapped messages but had not actually spoken since his arrival. "Sorry I missed your call. I don't get very good service at the house so I'm down here at the dock – one of the only places this seems to work!" He wanted to really talk with his father, but he clearly had to improve his timing. "Anyway, I'll try you later. O.K... Love you, Dad." He closed the cover on his Razr cell phone, put it in his pocket, and started to walk to his car.

It was about 10:30 a.m. and the ferry had just come in, creating a lot of bustle with people arriving and getting lined up to go off island at half past Noon. David looked around as he walked through the parking lot to his car, parked at the far end, near the street. He opened the door and started to get in, when he suddenly caught a glimpse of Angela in her white truck, driving toward the ferry ramp.

He strained to see what was happening, feeling every inch the voyeur. He soon enough spotted the young, dark haired Olivia as she opened the passenger door, got in, scooped up her puppy, and closed the door. The tinted glass obscured her from clear view, but David stood there, half in and half out of his car, and continued watching as Angela drove past. He got a better look at Olivia's face as the truck moved directly past his parked car, but Angela was quickly out of the parking lot, turning right onto Main Street and out of sight.

David got into his car and started the engine. He let a few trucks go by before pulling out of the parking spot. Something nagged at David, thinking about the girl. Turning onto Main Street, he couldn't shake the thought that there was something he was missing, and it had to do with Olivia.

Twenty-seven

Davcontinue had happily found a small stack of split, very well seasoned logs in the wood shed and now had a nice fire blazing in the kitchen stove. Earlier he had gotten the old oil space heater working, thanks to a delivery of kerosene and some expert advice from the proprietor of Brown's Boat Shop. He had also finally had some luck getting a contractor from Rockland on the phone, who had agreed to come out to the island within a few days to look over the job.

Feeling somewhat better than he had of late, David now stood in the dining room, looking over his mother's architectural plans that he had spread out on his make-shift table. He was eating a sandwich that he had picked up at the Islander, along with a fresh cup of coffee.

After he studied the plan carefully, he looked around the room, trying to match up some of the details. He took another sip of coffee and walked into the old parlor room looking at the walls. He opened a door along the East wall that he hadn't noticed before, and discovered a dark, closet-like space backing up to the central chimney. Interesting… David started to turn around and go back to the dining room when he noticed what looked like a small pile of books tucked in a dark corner.

Squatting down to take a closer look, he quickly saw that the top book was an old, dusty cook book. He put it aside carefully, trying not to stir up too much dust. The next book was an Old Farmer's Almanac Guide to Companion Gardening. He flipped through the pages for a minute before setting it on top of the cook book.

Next was a somewhat larger scrap book, dusty around the edges. David opened it and was surprised to see that the first page was a newspaper clipping dated July 14, 1960, with the bold heading "KENNEDY WINS NOMINATION". He turned the pages carefully and saw clippings and photos from the 1960 Presidential campaign, mostly featuring Jack Kennedy and his beautiful wife, Jackie, neatly organized and carefully pasted to each page. It was quite impressive, really, though it seemed to cover only the election and the very beginning of the Kennedy administration, with photos of the Kennedys in the White House, dating only into April, 1961. He closed the scrap book and carefully set it aside.

At the bottom of the pile he found an old photo album, with just a little dust around the edges. His knees were tired at this point, so David stood up to stretch his legs. He walked out of the dark, dusty enclosure and carried the album into the room which was now filled with sunlight. Propping the album on top of a box, he opened the cover carefully and started to flip through the pictures. The pages were black, and the photos were all black and white, dating back to 1920, according to the notes, carefully penned in white ink. Little black corner tabs held the pictures in place, though some were a bit loose. David slowly turned the pages, pausing occasionally to look more closely at photos that appeared to show the old farmhouse. He didn't recognize any of the people, but it was interesting to see the pictures of the house when it was a center of so much activity.

Toward the back of the book, David was abruptly taken aback to see a photo that looked familiar. Moving closer to the window as if being drawn to the light, David turned just enough to allow a ray of sunlight to shine directly on a photo Christmas card. This same photo had sat on his mother's piano for as long as he could remember! They had moved it only to make it part of the photo display for the funeral. It was the same black and white photo that had sat on the sideboard at his home after the funeral, showing a handsome family of four, Isabella and Randolph Winthrop, twelve year old Claire, and sixteen year old Randy, all smiling and happy.

The inscription, carefully written in white ink below the card, read "Christmas 1959". David very carefully pried the corners of the card out of the little black tabs and set the album back on the box, leaving it open to the now vacant page. He opened the card and found inside, below a typeset holiday greeting, a beautifully handwritten message:

> "Best Wishes for a Wonderful
> Christmas and a bountiful 1960!
> With gratitude and love,
> The Winthrop Family"

David closed the card and stared at the picture of his mother, strangely feeling more closely connected to his mother, yet voyeuristic at the same time.

~

David was in a really good frame of mind as he walked up the hill carrying a large box. He had reasoned that it was just easier to put the books in something to carry them up to show to Elsie, but he had to smile when he realized that he had, in his haste, grabbed the toilet tank box! She wouldn't read anything into that, he was sure, being the good, practical Yankee that she was. He rang the doorbell and was still smiling when Elsie opened the door.

The Morning Room was bright and airy, with lots of sun streaming in from the South, and David felt actually welcome for the first time. The box had been put on the floor beside the table, and Elsie had been horrified when he had produced the contents. The cook book and gardening book had been quickly dusted off and were now sitting in a small pile on the table. The scrap book was in front of Elsie, and the photo album was in front of David, opened to the page where he had carefully placed the Christmas card back in it's little corner brackets.

Elsie was smiling but, although David felt she was glad to have the books back in her possession, he also thought she seemed a little uneasy. Her hand was outstretched toward the album as though she would like to grab it, he thought, but he didn't offer to hand it over.

"I'm just embarrassed that I didn't have everything cleaned out of there..." Elsie said, trying to pass off her fluster.

David shrugged casually and shook his head. "It's O.K., really! I'm fascinated, actually," David assured her, gesturing toward the scrap book. "You did quite a nice job keeping pace with the Kennedy family..."

Elsie shifted back slightly and patted the cover of the scrapbook in an almost tender gesture. "Oh, Claire did this..." she demurred.

Twenty-eight

December 22, 1960

It was just days before Christmas and the snow blanked the countryside. A modest evergreen tree stood in the corner of the dining room over at Sunnyside, with bright balls and shiny tinsel hanging from it's reasonably symmetrical branches.

Claire was sitting at the big mahogany dining room table, intently working on a project. A scrap book was opened on the table in front of her, and she was gently pressing in place an image of Jackie Kennedy holding her new baby, John, Jr., in a flowing christening gown, a smiling John Kennedy standing by her side. A pair of scissors and a bottle of paper glue sat next to the scrap book. Several copies of "Life" magazine were scattered on the table, and the cover picture has been freshly cut out of the one dated December 19, 1960.

Elsie walked into the room carrying a beautifully wrapped Christmas gift. She smiled. "From your father," she announced, as she carefully placed it under the tree, then she immediately came over to admire Claire's handiwork. "My goodness! Look at what you've done!"

Claire looked up expectantly. "Do you like it?"

Elsie carefully closed the scrap book then started from the front, turning the pages slowly. She saw all the many clippings and photos from the recent 1960 Presidential campaign between Richard Nixon and John F.

"Jack" Kennedy. There were many photos of Jack Kennedy and his beautiful wife, Jackie, their young daughter, Caroline, and now the new baby, John Jr.. "My... My..." she said approvingly. "You've got this right up to date, young lady! The President and First Lady should hire you to be their official memory keeper!"

Claire beamed. "Do they really have such a person?"

"Oh, Lord!" Elsie exclaimed, knitting her brow slightly. "Well now, I'm not sure what they call them, but I know there are folks who put together these presidential libraries... You know, filled with photographs and important papers... to help people remember everything they did..."

Claire thought about it for a moment and brightened. "Did you know that Jackie actually *lived* in Paris? She went to school there... *Just* like I'm going to do..."

"Well, then..." Elsie said with a warm smile. "That's something to look forward to! I'll bet all your friends will be green with envy!"

"Well..." Claire responded reflectively, "They all want to *look* like Jackie, and *dress* like her... so I guess you're right..."

Elsie smiled. She was a Baptist, and her politics were staunchly Republican, foursquare behind the war hero, President Dwight D. Eisenhower, soon to be replaced by the young Senator from Massachusetts. "You know... she's a Democrat – *and* a Catholic – but I have to say that it is hard not to like Mrs. Kennedy, being so elegant and beautiful, and such a loving young mother..."

Claire smiled and looked thoughtfully, tilting her head to the side as she gently touched the picture of Jackie holding her new baby, John Jr., that she has just pasted in the scrap book. "She looks so... beautiful, holding her baby like that..."

Elsie put her hands on Claire's shoulders and gave her a little hug.

Twenty-nine

December 12, 2006

Elsie wiped a tear from her eye. "Oh, the tragedy poor Mrs. Kennedy had to suffer! Having her little baby die, then her husband — *shot down* like that! It was a blessing she died before John John's horrible airplane crash..." Her voice trailed off, her mind wandering further down this particular memory lane.

They were still sitting in the Morning Room, and Claire's political scrap book now lay open on the table in front of Elsie. "Surrounded by tragedy!" She said, shaking her head. She looked at David, pausing for a moment before continuing, speaking in a low, confidential tone. "In so many ways, like your dear mother..." she concluded, her eyes glistening with unshed tears. "I'm so sorry!" she cried, tears flowing freely now. "It just brings back such long lost memories..."

David shook his head in protest. "Please don't apologize! I understand..." He hesitated and cleared his throat, thinking that it might be a good time to change the subject. "About this photo album, though..." he began, "I just thought that maybe I could borrow it and make copies of some of the pictures that show the farmhouse, if that's O.K.?"

Elsie sat up straight, dabbing at her tears. "Well..." She cleared her throat. "I'm sure I could just *give* you some of those pictures..." she said, reaching toward the photo album. "Just let me see that..."

"Oh! No!" David protested, keeping his hands on the photo album. "I couldn't let you break up this great collection of old photos!" he continued earnestly. "All I want to do is *copy* a few of these…"

Elsie's arm remained outstretched across the table. "But why waste the money? I'm *sure* that I have duplicates of most all of them! Why, we never even *noticed* that old book was missing!"

David had started to flip slowly through the pages, looking at each photo quickly, before turning another page, determined to identify the photos he most wanted to copy. "Like this one…" he said, pointing to a lovely Summertime photo, labeled as a 1920 view, showing the South side of the old farmhouse, the woodshed off to one side, and two apple trees and some lovely wild daisies in the foreground.

He picked the album up and started to turn it around so Elsie could get a better idea of what he was looking for, but stopped short when a loose photo fell out onto the floor. Elsie moved to grab it but David picked it up first. It was a color photo of a small, dark haired girl with a radiant smile, sitting on the swing hung from the thick lower branch of an old, gnarly apple tree. David could make out the features of the old wood shed in the background, but the thing that got David's attention was that the child's face looked extremely familiar. "Is this my mother?" he asked, his face a study of absolute concentration.

Elsie reached her hand out again. "Let me see…" she demanded, in a tone that said she was not to be denied this time. David slowly handed over the photo, reluctant to let go of what he was sure was an image of his mother as a very young girl.

Elsie looked at it for just a second and shook her head. "No... No..." she concluded, quickly slipping the picture into the cook book. "We didn't have colored pictures back then!" She smiled at David as she patted the cover of the cook book. "No... This is just one of my little granddaughters."

David was disappointed, even though he realized as soon as she said it that it must be true. Reluctant to let go of the idea of it being his mother's image, he observed sadly, "Oh... She just had a *look*..."

Elsie fluttered her hands. "Oh! Kids *all* look alike at some point! I have a hard time telling them apart!"

"But..."

"Say!" Elsie brightened, turning on her best smile. "Can I interest you in a nice piece of my apple pie? She stood up without waiting for an answer and scooped all the books up from the table, taking them off into the kitchen. "Baked it fresh just this morning!" she proclaimed by way of inducement. "And I have *real* ice cream too!"

David smiled weakly, feeling a little like road kill. "Sure..." he responded, his eyebrows raised slightly in a quizzical expression. Clearly it was Elsie's turn to change the subject.

~

David had ended up having a warm slice of apple pie with a generous scoop of creamy chocolate ice cream, after which Elsie had forced him to accept a large wedge of pie-to-go and a hefty serving of roasted chicken and corn. He had barely been able to carry all the food and the photo album back down the hill!

The old kitchen stove was soon blazing hot, to the point that David was compelled to go into the pantry and try to open the window a crack, in an effort to allow a bit of fresh, cooler air into the room. He struggled, without success, then paused for a minute to look out and watch the water streaming through the dam as the tide was rapidly changing. It was interesting, he thought, how the ebb and flow of the water so easily created a pattern that somehow knit everything together here in a sort of comforting "normalcy".

He tried the window once more and was about to turn away when he noticed something moving. He wiped the window with his shirt sleeve to get a clearer view. It was Olivia with her puppy walking down the slope onto the dam.

David quickly turned and hurried out of the pantry.

~

Moments later, the front door opened and David stepped out, closing the door quickly behind him. He walked off, with single-minded determination, in the direction of the dam.

As he approached the knoll overlooking the rocky barrier, the sky appeared to be taking on a pink hue as the sun was just beginning to set. David paused at the top of the rise, then quickly continued down the narrow roadway.

The sound of the water rushing through the hand-crafted openings in the dam seemed to roar in his ears as he crossed the Mill Stream. Midway, he slowed his pace when he saw that Olivia was turned away from him, playing fetch with her puppy in the field just beyond the water, apparently unaware of his approach. David took a deep breath and tried to calm his racing heart, afraid that he might inadvertently startle the young girl.

She was about five foot two, David guessed, nearly the height his mother had been, though considerably thinner in her shape. David wondered if his mother had looked like this in her youth, and the image both comforted and unnerved him. He hesitated, hoping she would look up and notice him, without being startled. He was unsure of his voice for a minute or so, so composed himself before speaking. "Nice puppy!" he finally called out.

Olivia whirled around, clearly surprised. Her hair was a little wild, covering part of her face. She quickly bent down to scoop up her puppy, but the energetic little dog quickly eluded her grasp and ran over to investigate the stranger.

David smiled, realizing he had, indeed, alarmed the girl. "Oh... I'm sorry!" he assured her quickly. "I didn't mean to startle you..." He reached down and picked up the puppy, who was busy wagging his tail as he sniffed his pants. "He's a cute little fellow..."

As David stepped forward to hand over the puppy, Olivia pushed the hair away from her face and reached out to take her pet. "It's a girl," she replied firmly, though not impolitely.

David blinked as he looked at her face. "Oh... My mistake..."

Olivia stepped to the side as if calculating the best escape route. The color in the sky had deepened and reflected magnificently in the water on either side of the dam. "I have to go home before it gets dark…" she murmured.

"Of course…" David was almost certain he had said the words, as he stepped aside and let Olivia pass. He stood motionless and watched her carry her puppy past him, over the dam, and back up toward the road.

~

It was fully dark by the time David returned to the old farmhouse. He quickly burst into the front hallway, rushing as he took off his jacket and hung it carelessly on a hook by the door.

He moved swiftly into the dining room and opened the photo album, now sitting on his makeshift table. He stopped suddenly, then started flipping back and forth through the pages. He stopped where he was sure the photo Christmas card had been, but there was now nothing there, save for the notation "Christmas 1959" in white ink below the blank space.

David took a deep, deliberate breath and slowly turned the pages again, finding blank spaces here and there. He furrowed his brow as he looked at the altered pages, then turned his head and looked out the old dining room window, up toward the lights glowing from the new kitchen windows of the barn-style house up the hill.

Thirty

December 13, 2006

Freda was manning the cash register at the Islander the next morning when David paid for his coffee and muffin, part of his new morning ritual. The exchange was wordless, just a smile and a nod from each party.

Once outside, David got into his car and pulled out of the parking lot, turning left to go back to the farm-house, as usual. Suddenly he stepped hard on the brakes, made a quick U-turn in front of the Fuller Cemetery gate, and headed off in the other direction, toward the village.

At the ferry terminal, David had his wallet out already as he walked in and took his place in line at the ticket counter. "Can you take a look to see if I can get a reservation back on the 5:15 boat?" he asked Margaret, one of two ticket clerks he had encountered on the island.

She shook her head. "Sorry... All the reservations are gone... But you'll be able to get on, most likely, if you get your car back in line when the middle boat loads up."

David thought quickly. "All right... I guess I'll just have to wing it..." he decided and he handed Margaret his money.

~

David drove into the parking lot at the Pen Bay Medical Center and immediately found a space to park. He got out of the car and headed toward the entrance, taking long strides to cover the ground quickly.

Inside, he walked down the hallway to the Room 220 and stopped just outside the door. He could see that the little Brown family was gathered in the room, and he really did not want to disturb them. He first looked at Olivia, sitting next to her father. She was reading a book out loud. David was touched by the scene. He wondered, for the briefest moment, what it would have been like if his mother was laying in a coma like this.

He quickly shook off the thought and looked over at Angela, who sat across the room, knitting quietly. David shifted his gaze back to Olivia where it hung for several moments, before Angela put aside her yarn and needles and quietly made her way over to her daughter. Unsettled at the prospect that one or both of them might turn their head and see him standing there like a stalker, David backed away from the door and quietly walked back down the corridor, toward the elevator.

After a minute of whispered conversation, Angela picked up her handbag and did, indeed, turn and walk out of the room, also down the corridor, toward the elevator. At first the young man standing there, waiting for the doors to open, did not penetrate her consciousness, her focus on her own thoughts was so intense. But David noticed her right away, out of the corner of his eye, and he turned to face her squarely. "Hi!" he said, brightly but subdued. Honesty was the best policy, he quickly decided. "I came by to check on things, but I didn't want to disturb you," he explained. That was honest enough.

Angela quickly recovered from her shock, drawing a deep breath that almost left a smile on her face. "You startled me!" she demurred in a voice barely above a whisper. "I was just going to get a cup of coffee," she continued, feeling awkward.

"May I join you?" David asked, surprised by his offer as this had not been his original intention.

The elevator door opened slowly. "It's cafeteria coffee," she said, stepping into the waiting metal chamber, as if an apology was due, "but suit yourself..." she quickly added with a weak smile, glad, she realized, to have the company.

As hospital cafeterias go, this was no better, certainly, but no worse than most, though David wished he had time to run back to the coffee shop near the ferry termi- nal and bring something back to share with Angela. But it was what it was, and he felt grateful, indeed, that she had welcomed his invitation as they settled down at a table by the window, overlooking Penobscot Bay.

"I don't mean to be impertinent, but isn't he quite a bit older than you?" David asked in as gentlemanly a way as possible.

"Nine years," she replied. "That's not so much!" she added quickly in her defense.

David shrugged. "I guess not, but – and this is just idle curiosity, mind you – I'm surprised he wasn't already involved with someone while you were still growing up!"

Angela smiled. "Doesn't always work that way on the island," she countered as though keeping a private joke. "I mean, with such a small population, it's not like you've always got a lot to choose from!" she protested. "Anyway, for quite a long time, everyone knew Dougie had set his sights on the Poole girl – from New York – and I guess she kept him tied up while I was in school."

"What do you mean?"

"Well, she came every Summer, kept him wrapped around her little finger, giving him hope that she might break with her family and move here year-round, but she was apparently being pursued by one or two more eligible boys from her own set. She showed up here one year with a wedding party in tow." Angela looked out the window and fell silent.

"So, how did you two get together?" David asked, not wanting to lose the momentum of the conversation.

"I was working at the store and he finally noticed me..." she recalled, looking down and blinking back a tear. She cleared her throat and continued. "I had always had a crush on him – as long as I could remember – so it wasn't hard to be nice to him." She paused again, remembering what seemed like so long ago. "One thing led to another and, well, Olivia happened. He tried to do the right thing..." she summarized, her voice trailing off as she shifted her gaze back out the window.

"So, what happened?" David prompted, his voice gentle.

"It just didn't work," she said softly without turning to face him.

"I'm sorry," David said, "I'm not trying to pry..."

She turned now and looked at him, and David could see the tears welling up in her eyes. "I don't know why it didn't work," she said in a whisper. "I never understood why I couldn't make him happy..."

~

David sat in his little car, parked in line at the ferry terminal in Rockland, vowing to *always* get a reservation in the future. It was cold sitting there, even having had two cups of hot coffee. He rubbed his hands as he looked around and sighed.

His encounter with Angela had been much more than he had hoped for when he had so impetuously made the trip to Rockland. A bonus, really. A genuine gift. He rubbed his hands again and decided to count his blessings.

The fog horn sounded and David perked up, watching with somewhat detached interest as the ferry pulled into the dock and the activity at the terminal increased. He looked around again, then looked at his watch. It was 5:05 p.m. and there was no sign of Angela and Olivia.

Before long, the ferry agent took David's ticket and sent him down to the loading ramp, where he was immediately directed aboard the ferry. He found himself parked, once again, tucked in the forward corner of the bow. Having a small car, he decided, relegated him to superfluous ballast status; mere stuffing for the smallest available space.

He looked steadily in the rear and side view mirrors, inexplicably anxious to see the white truck. His couldn't reconcile his feelings precisely, but he recognized that he was more and more disappointed as he watched the vehicles load, and still there was no sign of Angela and Olivia.

David opened the car door and got out. He looked at his watch. It was 5:15 and the ferry crew was clearly making preparations to cast off. David started to get back in his car but stopped suddenly when he glanced back over his shoulder and saw a white truck at the head of the ramp. The crew waived it on and then quickly put the chain across the stern of the boat and raised the ramp. A light went on inside the truck and David could clearly see that it was Angela and Olivia. He stood there and watched until the light went out.

~

It was after 6:30 p.m. by the time David pulled up the narrow dirt driveway and parked next to the old farmhouse. The sky was completely dark, but clear and full of stars. David got out of the car and paused for a minute, glancing over toward Sunnyside. He imagined, as he slowly walked toward the darkened farmhouse, that, had it been a warm Summer month instead of a cold December evening, he would, without doubt, be walking through a field of fireflies flitting about in his path. Had his mother ever caught them when she Summered up here? He still couldn't visualize her fully here, but he had a feeling she had enjoyed every bit of nature this island provided.

As he approached the house, he could see faint wisps of smoke rising from the center chimney, and he thought to himself how glad he was that he had figured out the oil space heater. Upon reaching the kitchen door, David shifted the keys in his hand to expose the dead bolt key. He considered it for a moment, then turned and looked up the hill toward the glowing lights of the barn-style house.

~

It was midnight and the farmhouse was in complete darkness. David had earlier fallen into a fitful sleep, but he was now wide awake. A cloud had apparently moved by, and a new beam of moonlight shone in his window, illuminating his features.

He got up out of bed, drawn to the window by the brilliance of the full moon. Looking around at the island landscape, he at first thought there was a fresh layer of snow blanketing the ground, but he soon realized that it was nothing more than the soft illumination of the moonlight playing tricks with his eyes.

David was deeply moved by the otherworldly effect of the moonshine, but his mind quickly turned back to more pressing matters. He took a deep breath, letting the air escape slowly. "Mother..." he whispered to no one in particular.

Thirty-one

December 14, 2006

Gentle waves lapped the shoreline of the coastal town of Rockland. A lone seagull sat atop the tower of the ferry dock, backlit by the glow of the rising sun.

All was as it should be. The inner harbor was protected by the long breakwater, its lighthouse sitting proudly at the end. Beyond the glistening waters of the open bay were the silhouettes of the islands on the horizon, far away, yet ever present.

Further up the coast, at the Pen Bay Medical Center, a nurse walked down a quiet hospital corridor and entered Room 220. Douglas Brown still lay in a coma, and it was time to check his vital signs again, now that the morning shift had come on. The nurse looked at the monitor and recorded the blood pressure and pulse readings on the patient's chart, then deftly put the thermometer scope in his ear, and recorded his temperature as well.

The nurse put the chart back in the rack at the foot of the bed and turned to leave the room. With one foot out the door, she noticed the monitor activity abruptly intensifying. She turned back and approached the bed, her eyes scrutinizing the monitor.

Suddenly, Douglas opened his eyes. He blinked, trying to focus his vision, a befuddled look on his face. He reached up and grabbed the nurse's arm. She turned toward him, startled, then smiled broadly. "Well! Good Morning!" she said, her exceedingly white teeth catching his attention for a second. "I guess you decided to come back..."

He looked around, confused, and then looked into the nurse's big blue eyes. "Where am I?"

Thirty-two

December 14, 2006

David arrived at the Islander early the next morning, before the coffee was fully brewed. He waited patiently for the brew cycle to finish, filling a large cup quickly, as soon as the last drop fell from the filter cone. As he carefully pushed the edges of a cover down over the curled rim of the paper cup, he mulled over the items in the pastry display, a small assortment of fresh muffins and doughnuts. Angela was behind the counter, counting the change in her cash drawer.

David smiled and pointed at the fresh baked goods. "Did you bake these?" he asked, wishing he had something else to open a conversation with.

"Not hardly!" Angela chortled, clearly amused by the suggestion. "Freda still does all the baking."

David shrugged. "Well... I'll take two of them anyway... Hmmm... I guess I'll go with a couple blueberry muffins."

Angela put two muffins in a bag and set it down on the counter in front of David as he handed her a five dollar bill. "Here you go..." she said with a smile, quickly looking away when David smiled back. "Will that be it?" she asked, caution evident in her body language.

David nodded. "Yes... Thanks..." He accepted his change and dropped it in the tip cup. "Ummm... Is there any... improvement?"

Angela looked up startled. "What?"

"At the hospital..."

"Oh... No..."

David shrugged, unsure what to do next. "I'm sorry... Really..." He picked up the bag of muffins, and, without debating it with himself further, he blurted out, "How old is your daughter now?"

Angela was so stunned by the question, she simply answered it directly. "Thirteen... Just turned..." she said, blushing slightly.

"She must look like her father..." David ventured, uncertain how far he could go before Angela would bolt.

Angela picked up a strand of her red hair. "That's pretty obvious..."

David smiled, and pressed on. "Who does *he* look like?"

Angela shook her head and shrugged her shoulders. "Oh, gosh... I don't really know... He doesn't much look like anyone! He was certainly the best lookin' one of the lot... Just got lucky, I guess!" She smiled wistfully then lowered her eyes.

David shifted. "Well... Funny how that works..."

Angela stepped back and changed the subject. "I... I thought you were leaving..."

David shook his head, but a quizzical expression took over his face. "Leaving? No… Not just yet…"

Angela shrugged her shoulders quickly. "Olivia said you were buying a ticket at the ferry office this morning…" she explained. "She just *happened* to see you!" she was quick to add.

David smiled and cocked his head, thinking how fortunate it was that she had made this observation. "Well… I had to get a truck reservation," he explained. "I have a plumbing contractor coming over tomorrow from Rockland; It's apparently the only way I'm likely to get anything done at the farmhouse…"

Angela raised her eyebrows. "Oh… Well… Folks 'round here see it as Dougie's job; They just feel *funny* about stepping in… You know, like it might be taking something away from him…"

"Is *that* it?" David smiled, surprised by the revelation, though not at all shocked. "Well, I guess that explains why nobody on the island wants to help me!" He paused reflectively for a moment. "But, I need to get the work done, so I hope you and Olivia will try and understand."

"It's your property; You can do whatever you want."

David cleared his throat. "Well, since you brought it up, I *do* have a favor to ask…"

Angela looked uneasy. "What's that?"

David looked her in the eye. "Do you think…" he paused to rephrase the question. "Could you come by the farmhouse and give me some advice about... *various* things?"

Angela looked away. "I don't know..."

David persisted. "Look... The truth is, I have to go back to school soon, so I was just thinking I might *hire* you to be my on-site manager... You know... You could oversee the project for me..."

Angela looked back at him, clearly stunned. "Are you serious?"

David took a deep breath and smiled. "Yes... Absolutely! And I was also thinking that maybe we could fix up the old Carriage House and then perhaps get a few goats or some alpaca... Maybe Olivia would want a job managing them?"

Angela shook her head in disbelief. "Why would you do this?"

"I... I thought about what you said, and I..." David looked down for a brief moment as if to collect his thoughts. "I just realized that this is what Mother would want me to do..."

"I... I don't know what to say..."

"Just say you'll give it your full consideration, and that you'll come by later to talk with me about the details, O.K.?"

Angela's eyes grew misty. "Well... Things have been difficult with Dougie not able to pay child support..."

"I was afraid that might be the case..." David mused.

Angela blinked her eyes. "You're sure about this? I mean, are you really *sure*?"

David smiled briefly then looked at Angela with an entirely serious expression. "This was my mother's island. I know she would want to do the same thing and I..." he paused to swallow the lump that had risen in his throat. "I really want to do it, for her."

~

Elsie opened the door to find David standing there, an enigmatic smile on his face, a bag of muffins in one hand, and his coffee cup in the other.

"Good Morning!" he said, hoping he did not sound too nervous. This had seemed like such a good idea at four o'clock this morning, but he wasn't quite so sure now that he was standing here. "I think I owe you breakfast..." he said, lifting the bag of muffins like a ticket for admission.

Elsie had, of course, already eaten breakfast with her husband, still accustomed to getting on with the day before the crack of dawn. She graciously invited David in, however, and settled him at the breakfast table in the morning room, opposite her own chair and cup of tea. The muffins were now sitting on one of Elsie's little plates, and David had a fresh cup of coffee in a ceramic mug.

Elsie settled down finally and clapped her hands. "Well, this is a nice surprise..." she said with an uncertain smile.

David nodded his head and smiled back at her, barely hearing her words, feeling as though he was ready to burst. "Good... Good..." He took a deep breath. "Mrs. Brown?"

"Yes?"

David cleared his throat. "I... I don't know quite how to ask you this, so please forgive me..." He paused and looked at her as she quietly studied him. "I'm just trying to... understand..."

Elsie's expression turned apprehensive. "What is it, dear?"

"Did..." David cleared his throat once more. "Did you and my grandfather..." He looked directly in her eyes and tried again, determined to spit it out. "Did you and my grandfather... have... have an affair?"

Elsie's expression turned to shock. "What?!! Oh, good Lord! No! Why in the world would you ask me such a thing?"

David shook his head, deeply disappointed that everything he thought he had finally figured out might not be so, nearly losing his nerve for a moment. "I'm sorry... I just..."

"Never!" Elsie sputtered. "Why the idea..."

David recalled that Elsie had not been candid with him about Angela, so he regained his purpose and plowed on. "I just... Well, the *truth* is... I... I just realized in the last day or so that *your granddaughter* – Olivia – looks *just* like *my mother* did! *Just* like that picture on the Christmas card..."

Elsie's looked down at her tea cup. Her hand was trembling. "You must be mistaken..." she said softly.

"No! No! And I know you know I'm right!" David insisted, his confidence growing as he recalled another clue. "I mean, you took my mother's pictures out of that album..."

"You... You just wanted pictures of the farmhouse..." Elsie protested.

"Please! I'm *not* making an *accusation*, Mrs. Brown," David quickly countered, softening his tone. "I am just... *trying* to understand; It would explain *a lot* if I knew he was my mother's half brother."

Elsie shook her head vigorously. "No! I was *never* unfaithful to my husband! Never! Why the very idea..."

"Then how do you explain..."

"You are mistaken!" Elsie interrupted, standing up as if to walk away. "I can't talk about this! I can't..."

"Please! Mrs. Brown!" David was desperate for her to tell him the truth. His mind raced. "I *know* you know more than you're telling me! Please don't make me have to resort to DNA testing to figure this out!" He wasn't sure at all about DNA, or how he would go about making good on his threat, but it just fell out of his mouth.

Elsie stopped and sat back down, looking directly at David, fear registering clearly in her expression. "DNA?"

David was encouraged. "Yes!" He groped for a convincing follow-up. "The science has advanced greatly, Mrs. Brown… DNA testing would answer *all* these questions…"

Elsie felt a sudden surge of defeat. She could not believe it had come to this, and she suddenly knew that she could not continue this battle. She got up slowly, without uttering a word, great anxiety etched on her face. With slow deliberation, she walked, not without hesitation, into the dining room.

Pausing for a moment when she finally reached the sideboard, Elsie slowly opened a drawer, shuffled a few things, and pulled out the photo Christmas card. She stood silently for a moment and looked at it as tears rolled down her face. David watched all this expectantly, afraid to speak.

Elsie turned and slowly walked back to the Morning room, her eyes casting a veil of gloom, overshadowing the brilliant sunshine that was streaming in through the windows. She sat back down at the table, opposite David, and slowly, with great deliberation, handed him the Christmas card. "Look closely…" she instructed, her voice barely audible. David took the card and looked at it. "Who does your mother look like?" Elsie prompted, wiping at her tears with the corner of her apron.

David wrinkled his brow. "Well… She looks like Olivia…"

"No!" Elsie corrected him sharply. She paused and took a long breath. "Look at your grandmother," she instructed, her voice once again soft.

David looked perplexed. He looked at Elsie for a moment, then focused again on the card. "She looks like my…"

"Your mother…" Elsie sighed, completing his sentence for him. "Your mother looks exactly like *her* mother!" She looked David straight in the eye. "Your *grandfather* had *nothing* to do with that."

David was confused. "So, how did *your* son have a daughter who looks like my mother?"

Tears rolled down Elsie's cheeks. She reached for a tissue and dabbed at her eyes. "He's… He's *not* my son…" she choked out.

"What?" David thought he had misunderstood.

Elsie wiped at her face, desperately trying to regain control. She sat up straight. "I berthed him… I held him in my arms before anyone else…" she said with pride, "and I *raised* him like a son…"

"What are you saying?" David's head was spinning. He had come here thinking that he had it all figured out, but now he was more confused than ever.

Elsie looked at him pleadingly. "Please understand," she begged. "I *love* him every bit like a son…" She looked away and shook her head sadly. "But I did *not* give birth to him."

"What?" David was uncomprehending. "Then, who…?"

"Oh, my... I..." a fresh batch of tears flowed from Elsie's eyes. "I gave my word I would take it to my grave!" she cried.

"What are you *talking* about?" David asked, thoroughly perplexed.

"I never..." Elsie shook her head, "*never* thought I would break my *promise*... I..." She paused and took a fresh tissue, blinking as she wiped at her face. "I *understand* that I have to tell you now; I can't let you drag everyone through all that DNA business, but please!" She looked at David and reached out to touch his hand. "Please try and understand! Things were more... more *complicated* back then..."

"What?" David struggled to make sense of what he was hearing. "Are you trying to tell me that he's my *grand-mother's* son?" he asked, incredulously. "That makes no sense..."

Elsie shifted uncomfortably, then looked directly back at David, shaking her head wearily. "No... No... That's not it..." She looked down at her hand. "Oh... Dear!" She closed her eyes and took a slow, deep breath. "I... I *think* your mother *might* have told you at some point..." She looked up at David again. "I don't know..." She quickly looked down at her tea cup. "I don't know... She probably would have eventually told you that..." she blinked and looked back into David's eyes, "that you have an older brother."

Shock registered on David's face. "Brother! What?" he pushed away from the table. "How... How can I have a brother?"

"Oh, dear..." Elsie started to weep again. "You're *so* young! I suppose... things are different these days... But back then, it wasn't so... *simple*..."

David shook his head vigorously. "No! It isn't possible!"

Elsie nodded. "He *is* your brother, David; He's your mother's natural child..."

David's body rocked back in disbelief and shock. "That's crazy! How could my mother have a forty-five year old son?"

Elsie wrung her hands in dismay. "But it's true! Oh... Dear!" She closed her eyes for a moment, shaking her head sadly. "This was such a mistake..."

"No! I don't believe you!" David's voice had grown louder. "You're lying! There is no way! It just can't be true!"

Elsie wiped her eyes as she shook her head. "But, David... You *saw* her yourself! I would *never* have broken my promise to your mother and grandfather! But you *saw* the truth in little Olivia!" She leaned forward, raising her voice. "You *made* me tell you! You threatened me with DNA! Why would I tell you a lie?!"

David stood up and stepped back from the table, his thoughts spinning. How could he trust what this woman was saying? "Why all the secrecy?" he demanded. "Why hide the photos? Why..."

They suddenly heard a bumping noise. David turned and looked at the foyer as Elise wiped frantically at the tears on her face. The front door opened and Samuel came in, taking off his rubber boots before moving into the room.

As he walked through the seating area, headed in the direction of the dining room, Samuel took note of David, standing now by the windows on the East side of the Morning Room. "Everything O.K. in here?" he queried, looking from David to Elsie.

Elsie forced a big smile and spoke up quickly. "Oh... Yes! Just fine!"

"What did you say?" Samuel asked, turning his good ear toward his wife and straining to hear better.

"David here just brought by some fresh muffins..." Elsie said loudly, lifting the plate of muffins for him to see.

Samuel shook his head and lifted a hand in protest. "No thanks! Don't want to spoil my dinner!"

Elsie looked at the clock. "You're back a little early," she observed loudly.

"Have to use the facilities..." Samuel responded, confidentially. He turned to look at David and pointed to a chair. "Make yourself at home," he instructed with a smile, then he turned and walked off through the dining room. Elsie and David remained motionless until they heard him close the door to the Master suite. Elsie looked at David and motioned to the chair. "Please..."

David stepped closer but continued to stand. "Does *he* know?" he asked, his voice low.

"Who? *Sam?*" Elsie responded. "Of course Sam

knows!" she continued emphatically, without raising her voice. "Good Lord, I'd have to be pretty slick to fool *him* on that score!"

"So who else knows?" David pressed.

Elsie blinked her eyes for a moment. "Why... nobody..."

Thirty-three

September 10, 1960

It was the first weekend after Labor Day, and for many on the tiny island it represented the best of all worlds. The weather was perfect; as good as or better than any day in August. Furthermore, and more to the point, the majority of the Summer residents, especially those having to pack children off to school, were long gone, back to their homes in Connecticut, New York, or wherever.

It was not that the Summer residents were not welcome; Islanders knew that much of their livelihood was now derived from their affiliations with those two-thousand plus who merely vacationed on their soil. It was just that they, by and large, were most content during the nine or ten months of the year when their numbers topped off around three-hundred or so; When life was more balanced.

Now, the charming Sunnyside, sitting proudly above the Mill Stream, was surrounded by flower gardens that had mostly passed by, though there were asters and a few hardy mums still in flower. There was a single, 1960 model Cadillac parked by the small barn, the door of which was closed now, and bolted shut, preventing any chance encounter with Isabella's Jaguar, a birthday gift that had brought her joy for all too brief a period of time.

The laughter and gaiety of many past Summers had long since ceased to make their presence known here.

Nothing really could be done to erase the bleakness that had settled on the place since that fateful day in early July.

Elsie, forty years old, walked up the long, winding driveway, crossing over the stone dam, looking neither right nor left, headed directly to the kitchen door.

~

Claire was in Elsie's arms, crying great pitiful sobs of despair into her broad shoulder. Her father, forty-seven year old Randolph, stood ashen-faced by the table, holding onto the back of a chair. He cleared his throat and shifted his feet uncomfortably. "Claire..." he said, gently but sternly, "go along to your room, now, so I can talk with Mrs. Brown".

"I want to stay..." Claire cried, not looking at her father.

Elsie gave her a hug and took out a handkerchief. Gently and with great maternal love, she started dabbing at Claire's wet face. "Now... Run along like your father said..." she commanded, soothing but stern, her voice almost a whisper. "I'll come along by and by and visit with you when we're done here, O.K.?"

Claire looked at her as if for reassurance. "O.K...."

Elsie smiled and dabbed a bit more at the tears flowing down the girl's cheeks, then gave her another loving hug. Claire pulled away and slowly walked toward the doorway to the main part of the house, glancing sadly at her father as she passed him. Elsie shook her head as she watched Claire leave the room.

"Poor thing..." Elsie observed. "The heartache she's

been through since that horrible accident in July... Now *this*..." Her gaze now rested squarely on her employer.

Randolph sighed deeply and shook his proud head. "Elsie... I am just *beside* myself... *Nothing* has gone right since... since that *awful* day when my Isabella... Well..." He paused and looked sorrowfully at Elsie. "I am *so* sorry for involving you in our troubles, but I *know* I can trust you to help me protect Claire... Protect the family name... This has to be *absolutely* confidential..."

Elsie was troubled by her employer's request. "But, what about Sam?... and John? Dad and Chester are not a problem, and I can protect her from the folks in the village... and anyone else who happens to be around off-season, but..."

Randolph looked down for a moment. "Yes... I've thought about that..." He looked back at Elsie. "You might recall that I had offered to send John to trade school..."

Elsie was surprised by the introduction of this old promise into the conversation at hand. "Well... Yes... We talked about sending him off to learn a trade in a couple of years... after he graduates high school..."

Randolph raised his hand and nodded. "Well... Yes, that's true, but I can place him in a good private school right *now*..." He looked at Elsie for her reaction, then pressed on. "In central Massachusetts... tuition... room and board... and I will arrange a school trip in December... a *special* trip to Disneyland for the *whole* group from school... John will be a *hero* with his classmates... and he won't have time to come home for Christmas this year... There won't be any questions..."

Elsie was stunned by the thoroughness of Randolph's plan. "But... John's never been away from the island! A night here or there in Rockland, but never *away*..."

Randolph had no other ideas. He had to convince her. "But it will be a *great* opportunity for him to really make something of himself... and... and John can come home for Spring break... I've given this a lot of thought! The..." he stopped to clear his throat. "The baby is due sometime in the beginning of April..." He paused, looking almost pleadingly at Elsie. "After you... *birth* her... I'll arrange to get her out by boat... Take her right down the Mill Stream after dark and onto my boat in Pulpit Harbor; Nobody will even notice... I'll sail up the coast and transfer to shore in Bar Harbor, then we'll fly to Paris..."

Elsie's head was spinning. All these details! "But... What about her schooling?"

"She's very bright..." Randolph responded immediately, clearly having thought this out as well. "You can school her while she's here, and she'll be able to get right back into the swing of things when she gets to the private school over there..." He could see that Elsie was uncertain. "*Please*, Elsie... I can't let this ruin her life..."

Elsie shook her head. There was another detail that had not been discussed. "But... But what about the baby?"

Randolph took a step closer to Elsie, lowering his tone. "I'll... I'll arrange it so you can sign the birth papers... You know... as your *own*... with Sam as your witness – it will all be legal – and you and Sam can raise the child..."

Elsie shrank back, shaking her head slowly. "Oh... I don't know, Mr. Winthrop... Sam and I work hard to get by as it is... A baby would be a big..."

"I'll take care of you..." Randolph quickly assured her. "I *promise*... I'll cover all of John's education, and... and I'll increase Sam's pay... And yours..."

"I don't know..." Elsie was still shaking her head. "I'll have to talk to Sam..."

Randolph was desperate. "I'll sign over the farmhouse across the way... Your house... the barn... all the land... I'll deed it to you and Sam..."

"Mr. Winthrop..." Elsie protested weakly. "I... Please don't misunderstand... I want to help, but a baby is a mighty big commitment..."

"I don't know who else to turn to, Elsie!" Randolph pressed, afraid to let her go without an agreement. "I know how much Claire trusts and loves you... You're like family!"

Elsie was moved. "Mr. Winthrop... You *know* I love that little girl like my own child..." She looked sympathetically at Randolph's tragic stricken face, then sighed heavily. "All right... All right... I promise... I'll take care of Claire... like you said... I'll talk to Sam... So long as you make things right – like you said – I think he'll be willing to go along..."

Thirty-four

December 14, 2006

Davidavid was stunned. He sat, leaning forward, intently focused on Elsie's face. "So, my grandfather *bought* your silence?"

"No! It wasn't like that!" Elsie protested. "You… You have to try and understand!" She paused, trying to gather her thoughts. "I know these days young women seem to think *nothing* of having babies without being married, and nobody bats an eye, but it was *different* back then! Something like this…" She shivered. "Well, a girl would be disgraced! Your grandfather had no choice! He had to protect his little girl *and* her good name – but, at the very same time, he had to make sure that his grandchild was provided for – and *protected* – even if he wouldn't be raised a Winthrop…" Elsie looked sadly at David, tears glistening in her eyes.

"This was not an easy thing he asked of us…" she continued. "He didn't *"buy"* our silence, but he provided for us so we could raise the *child*…" Elsie took a deep breath and added, "and, yes, John went off and got a good education, and, yes, Mr. Winthrop signed the farmhouse over to us – Sam and me; It was the *right* thing to do…"

David was confused again. "But my *mother* owns this property…"

"Well, *now*, she does," Elsie confirmed. "But, back then, Mr. Winthrop was good as his word."

David struggled to understand. "So... My mother just hid here with you? How old was she?"

"Oh... Let's see now..." Elsie searched back through her memory. "Douglas was born on April 15, 1961... Claire was fourteen – just turned, when she had him..."

"She was fourteen?" David asked to be clear. "That was *rape* you know!"

Elsie looked shaken. "Oh, dear! Well... Yes, I suppose... I never really thought about it that way; We... we just wanted what was best for Claire..."

"But, who *did* this to her?" David pressed. "Who's the father?"

"I... I don't know..." Elsie confessed. "Claire never would say. It upset her, so I stopped asking..." She looked down and let out a deep sigh. "I always had my suspicions, of course, but... well... I guess I kept them to myself now long about forty-six years, so there isn't much point giving them breath at this late date..."

David shook his head, still reeling from all these revelations. "But, you *raised* him as your own son! Don't you want to *know* who his father is?"

Elsie shook her head. "I stopped thinking about it long ago... It doesn't matter, really... It surely wouldn't change anything..."

David thought for a moment. "Does my grandfather know?"

Elsie looked out the window. "I suspect so..."

"And Doug..." David continued. "Did *he* know?"

"Oh, no! No, no, no..." Elsie looked back at David.

"And what about all the financial things my grandfather and mother did for you... Nobody ever asked why?"

Elsie looked thoughtful for a moment. "Why? Well... It was just the Winthrop way of caring for their own. We were like family..."

"So, *nobody* knows about this except you and Mr. Brown, my mother, and my grandfather?" David pressed again.

"And now *you*..."

"And now me..."

Elsie leaned in toward David and spoke in confidential tones. "We promised to keep Claire's secret, and that was that. There was no need to ruin her life more than it had been already; We did it to protect her. Everyone kept their word... At least..." A troubled expression crept onto her face. "At least, right up until now..."

David thought for a moment. "What about *him*? Do you think Mother might have told him?"

"Told *who*?"

"You know... Is it possible that she told *him*... the truth about his birth?"

"*Douglas?*"   Elsie considered the question carefully. "Oh... I forgot about that... I... I don't *know* if she did it... Oh, my..."

Thirty-five

November 22, 2006

John's wife, Mollie, was doing the big meal this year, but Elsie had insisted on baking her famous apple pie as her contribution to the Thanksgiving feast. To that end, she had her long apron on and was busy cutting up apples, slicing them thin and coating them thoroughly with her secret mix of sugar and spice before arranging them neatly in the pie plate, perfectly lined by her made-from-scratch buttermilk pie crust. In her usual, efficient way, Elsie had everything neatly arranged on the counter, and the top crust had already been rolled out neatly between two sheets of wax paper.

The jarring sound of the phone ringing broke the productive quiet of the room. Elsie put down the knife and the apple she had been about to quarter, wiped her hands on a kitchen towel, and walked toward the wall telephone to pick up the handset. "Hello?"

Claire's voice was clear over the phone. "Elsie! Good morning!"

"Claire!" Elsie was pleased to hear her voice. "I *just* put a little note in the mail, to you! How are you?"

"Good... Good..." Claire's voice trailed off for a moment. "Things are good here..."

Elsie smiled. "I'm so glad..."

"Elsie…" There was silence on the line for a moment. "I wanted to talk with you about something…"

Elsie's smile faded. "Oh…"

Back in Westport, Claire was in her beautiful kitchen, standing near the side window, pacing slightly as she talked on the phone. Occasionally she would look out the window toward the guest house, as if waiting to see someone come out. "I need to ask what you think about something, Elsie…" She paused again, absentmindedly twisting the phone cord. "I… I am thinking… that I… I should *tell* him…"

Elsie took a sharp breath. "Oh… I don't know, Claire… After *all* these years…" The voice on the phone trailed off for a moment. "It's up to you, of course… But… But *why*?"

Claire shook her head and shrugged. "I don't know… I… I keep running this round and round in my head and I just think I might be able to *help* him more if he knew…"

Elsie fiddled mindlessly with her apron as she sat on the stool by the wall phone, a worried expression on her face. "I don't know…" she sighed. "We've kept this all this time… It could do more harm than good at this point… But it's up to you…"

Thirty-six

December 14, 2006

"Do you remember the letter you brought me?" Elsie asked David, tears running down her cheeks. "Douglas wrote it that same morning – the day of the *accident* – and he *clearly* didn't know when he wrote it; I'm sure of that..." Elsie's voice trailed off as she got up and crossed to the sideboard. She opened the drawer and pulled out an envelope. "You can see for yourself..." she asserted, but she also wanted to re-read the letter to assure her own mind.

She pulled the letter out of the envelope as she walked back to the table, and started reading it. "He wrote about how nice Claire was," she summarized, "how grateful he was for the work, but that he felt out of place and would be happy to be home again..." She handed the letter to David. "...with his *own* family when the job was done..."

David looked at the letter and considered what Elsie had told him about the phone call. "But, you *do* think Mother *planned* to tell him?"

Elsie dropped her head forward and absently rubbed her hand on her forehead, anxious to remember everything about her conversation with Claire. She lifted her head and her gaze wandered out through the window, fixing on a lone tree across the field, a tortured expression on her face as she blinked back tears. "I think she might have done it..." she whispered. "I should have just said 'No'..."

The phone rang suddenly, breaking the near silence of the room like an urgent fire alarm sounding in a quiet library. Elsie jumped, then she got up as quickly as possible, dabbing at her tears as she walked toward the kitchen. She cleared her throat before she answered the phone. "Hello... Oh, hello! Oh, my... Yes... Yes, of course."

Elsie hung up the phone and slowly turned toward David. "He's coming..."

~

David left the barn house in a daze, his mind running on overload. He got into his car and drove down the hill, as if on automatic pilot.

He parked next to the old farmhouse and got out, closed the car door, then walked North, over the rise, across the road, and down the hill toward the water. As he walked onto the dam, he paused to look downstream, then he turned and looked up at Sunnyside, transfixed by the images he now saw plainly.

Thirty-seven

December 14, 2006

T he hospital curtain was deftly whipped open by a tall, middle-age nurse, and left hanging loosely from the ceiling track, far enough back to fully reveal the patient and doctor finishing up their encounter.

Douglas Brown was sitting in the chair by the bed, looking well rested but weary. He was not giving any heed to the physician, but was, instead, now thinking with a singular mind about his situation and how he had arrived there. The doctor finished writing something on the patient chart, then turned and smiled at Douglas. "Well, I can only say once again how *remarkable* it is that you are sitting here, awake... and so lucid..." he said, his voice betraying a measure of unwarranted self satisfaction.

Douglas did not smile in return, but looked at the doctor with a very serious expression on his face. "I have to go home..." he responded in a flat tone, as though he had heard nothing the doctor had just said.

The doctor was momentarily taken aback, having, perhaps, expected a laudatory expression of some sort from his new prize patient. He recovered quickly and shook his head, smiling as he put the chart back in the rack at the foot of the bed. "Well, we have to take things one step at a time now..."

Douglas shook his head. "But I think there's something important I need to take care of..." he said, looking out the window toward the open waters of the ocean that separated him from the island.

~

The Rockland ferry terminal was busy, though not nearly as busy as it would be in a couple of months, once the cold winds of Winter had given way to late Spring breezes.

Looking, and feeling, a little out of place, Randolph's attendant stood patiently in line at the ticket window for the North Island ferry, waiting for the clerk to sort out a problem with a missing reservation.

By the time he got to the window, he was ready to get right down to business. "Round trip, car and driver; One passenger one-way, please," he requested, handing over a crisp fifty dollar bill.

~

As the ferry entered the Thoroughfare and approached the dock, the captain looked down at the deck, mildly curious as to why the classic 1960 Cadillac limo, looking oddly out of place among the trucks and modern sedans, was sitting mid deck, on its way to the island. Maybe one of the more eccentric inhabitants had arranged for an elegant limo ride to celebrate a birthday, or anniversary – but where the hell would they ride to? No, that wasn't it, but he'd sure find out soon enough; Of that he was certain.

~

David stood in the kitchen of the old farmhouse, watching out the window as Randolph's car slowed to a near halt before it turned left to travel over the dam and slowly up the winding driveway, pulling directly up to the front of the house.

The front door opened and Elsie stepped out, a sweater thrown hastily over her shoulders, wiping her hands on her apron. She waited expectantly by the door as the attendant emerged from the car and took a wheelchair from the trunk.

Thirty-eight

December 15, 2006

One might be tempted to describe the living room at Sunnyside as a warm and thoroughly comfortable space in which to relax, or a veritable haven which boasted beautiful vistas upon which to gaze and furnishings that embraced you in an elegant, timeless style. Decorated many years ago by the formidable Mrs. John Winthrop, and subsequently enlivened by the beautiful Isabella Winthrop, the room remained charming and neat, with everything perfectly in place, just as they had been since 1960 or before.

It had been many years since any Winthrop had been in residence, but when he was brought in the front door, Randolph had been washed with the feeling of coming home.

He had remarried, during that most difficult year, some months after he had laid his son to rest next to Isabella. Elisabeth had comforted him, and organized him, and he had been grateful for her guidance throughout that lost and lonely time. She was a good woman and he had provided well for her in life. In nearly forty faithful years of marriage he had not, however, even once let her come to this place. North Island belonged to Isabella.

Yes, he had dutifully bought a double plot in Boston, and Elisabeth now lay there beneath a great marble stone which honored her and bore his name, but he had no intension of being buried anywhere except next to his beloved first wife.

Wearing a white dress shirt and handsome red cardigan sweater, Randolph now sat in a beautiful wing back chair, with an ottoman under his legs and a blanket draped over his lap. Elsie had prepared some fresh hot tea before she went back across the way. The slender ceramic tea pot sat on a matching ceramic trivet, within easy arm's reach on the small round table beside him. An elegant tea cup and saucer sat close to the edge, filled with the steaming amber liquid, next to a delicate plate with a half eaten biscuit. Elsie meant well, Randolph knew, but his hunger was not so easily satisfied.

He yearned for the past. He was hungry only for all that he had lost. So many times he had relaxed here, in this very chair, while Isabella fussed about with the children or sat happily on the sofa next to him, talking about the day or planning her next social event. So many happy times...

He sighed deeply and turned his head to look out the window, a sorrowful, somnolent expression fixed like a mask on his face as he surveyed the lovely landscape, sloping gently away toward the water. He could see the old 1830 farmhouse as it sat proudly defiant in the distance, on the rise above the roadway. The new barn-style house, sitting further up the hill, to the right, looked familiar in it's shape and size, though he had never seen it until this day. Claire had surely been saddened to hear that the old barn had collapsed; She had done a fine job reconstructing it, in a manner of speaking, a bit further up the hill.

Randolph was roused from his solitary thoughts by a

loud knock at the door. He sat up straight and blinked his eyes, but he did not turn his head toward the sound. Moments later, he heard different sounds as his attendant opened the door. Never turning his head from the window, he knew that his grandson, David, was standing there, undoubtedly sporting a serious look on his face.

~

David felt torn: On the one hand, he was amazed to be walking, for the first time, where his mother had spent so many hours as a child, and he wanting to feel it completely, absorbing as much as possible from the experience. On the other hand, he knew he was here, at this moment, to wrestle decades old details out of an old man he barely knew, and that fact, a conundrum in itself, had only recently come into focus.

How had it been that all his life he had never even once felt the absence of his mother's father? Of course he knew that holidays and vacations had centered around his father's parents in Connecticut, with whom he and Amie had shared a great many wonderful moments through the years. Yet he could recall not a single moment when he had even thought to question why they never spent time in Boston, or why his grandfather never spent time in Westport. It seemed absurd, looking back, but only in the rear view mirror. Obviously his mother had deliberately created a world for her family that was so complete, no one had ever noticed that something was missing.

After exchanging a terse preliminary greeting, David settled himself, somewhat uncomfortably, on the long sofa, at a right angle to his grandfather. Regarding him closely, he marveled again at how this man could be a virtual stranger to him, in spite of his age. Why had they never spent any time together? Why couldn't he remember even a single holiday or event where he had enjoyed more than a glancing opportunity to know this man? Why had his mother not encouraged a warmer relationship? David swallowed and cleared his throat for good measure before speaking again. "Grandfather?"

Randolph looked sadly at his grandson. "David..."

David shifted uneasily, trying to think of some appropriate small talk, but when he opened his mouth again, the first thing he said was what had been on his mind all day, "Why did you come?"

Randolph tilted his head as an almost imperceptible smile flitted across his withered face. "I think I might ask you the same..."

David berated himself silently for handling this so badly, but quickly answered the question. "Mother had planed to restore the farmhouse across the way. I... I want to see it through... for her..."

"She *talked* to you about it?" Randolph asked, his curiosity clearly piqued.

David shrugged and shook his head. "No... She *never* talked to us about this place at all; I found the plans after... the funeral..."

Randolph nodded his head in understanding. "I see..."

David looked at his grandfather for a moment before

continuing uneasily. "I've actually... *discovered* quite a few things since... then..."

Randolph leaned forward, ever so slightly. "You've been talking to the Browns?"

David felt his heart racing and he could hardly breathe. "Yes..." he responded softly, then cleared his throat and continued in a stronger voice. "Yes, and I... I really need to ask you a few questions... about Mother..." his voice trailed off as he seemed to run out of air.

Randolph leaned back again and slowly picked up his tea cup. "What do you want to know?" he asked, looking over the brim of the tea cup before taking a sip and shakily putting the cup and saucer back on the side table.

David waited until the cup was back in place and Randolph's eyes were focused on him again. "Well... I... I want to know what happened in 1960... After my grandmother's boating accident? I... I really need to know..." David paused to clear his throat again, clearly uncomfortable with what he was about to ask. "Well... The question is: *Who* is Douglas Brown's real father?"

Randolph looked stricken and defeated at the same time. Elsie had not warned him that his grandson could be so direct. He leaned forward and reached out with a shaky hand to touch David's arm. "I'm so sorry I never really got to know you, David..."

He paused and closed his eyes for a moment, then opened them and looked directly into David's eyes. "I've been alive for *ninety-two* years now; The first half was truly *outstanding*; I could *not* have asked for more..." Randolph bowed his head for a moment, then lifted it and continued looking at David. "The last half... The last half has been filled with nothing but great sorrow and endless regrets; Not really knowing you and your sister chief among them..."

David was shaken by this preamble, feeling somehow guilty, but at the same time frustrated that his question was not being answered. "Grandfather..." He stopped and looked around the room for a moment. Spotting a group of photos across the room, he stood and walked over to an antique drop-leaf table and picked up a beautifully framed picture of a young Claire sitting on a dock, smiling radiantly, her legs dangling, her hair pulled back in a ponytail. He carried the photo back to Randolph and pointed to it. "My mother... *Please* tell me what happened to my mother..."

As Randolph reached out to touch the photo, the tremors in his hands increased. "I came back here to die..." he said, barely above a whisper, seemingly ignoring David's question. "If *I* had been in that boat instead of her... My beautiful Isabella..."

David shook his head vigorously, afraid that his grandfather's mind is now wandering. "No! No, Grandfather! This is your daughter... Claire... My mother..."

Randolph nodded his head as he looked at the photo. "I know..." he responded solemnly. "Claire... She was so *much* like her mother..."

The room fell silent and David waited, looking uneasily at his grandfather before speaking again. "Tell me about 1960," he prompted urgently. "Grandfather... *Please*... Tell me what happened to my mother..."

Randolph squinted his eyes and looked at David.

"Why do you need to know?" he asked, his head starting to tremble. "How can it *possibly* make any difference?"

David's heart was beating like it would pound right through his chest. "Because I *need* to understand how Doug fits into my mother's life!" He exploded. David shook his head and continued, lowering his voice. "Because I have gone *round* and *round* and I can *only* conclude that the *darkness* which surrounds his very life is somehow responsible for putting him in a position to *kill* her!" David took a step closer and lowered his voice another decibel. "Because my mother is *in* the ground, but her soul is reaching out to me to understand why she is no longer here to welcome me home, or laugh at my stories... or thrill to the beauty of a sunset..." David concluded, gesturing toward the window, his eyes glistening with emotion.

Randolph shifted his gaze to look out the window again. Tears filled his eyes as he watched the sunset gracefully transform into a decidedly more vibrant display. "Everything changed..." he started, shaking his head. "The accident... It *never* should have happened..." Randolph paused to wipe tears from his eyes. "They looked for days..." he continued. "Everyone *said* it was hopeless, but..." He sat up straight and let out a loud deep breath. "But I *couldn't* accept it; I *believed* she would come back to me!"

David was moved by his grandfather's obvious grief, but he pressed for an answer. "But, what happened to *my* mother?"

Randolph shook his head slowly. "It was a mistake... It never should have happened..." He took a deep breath, then paused, gazing back at the sunset. David scrutinized his face but did not break his silence.

"Everything was wrong!" Randolph finally continued, his voice grave and choked with emotion. "It was... It was just as if the skies had opened up... and... the *whole* sky – the *universe* really – was *replaced* by these... *flowing* lights... of every color, all around..." He paused, closing his eyes for a moment before continuing. "I looked up... and there she was! My Isabella! In her dinner dress..."

David shook his head. His grandfather was mixing things up. He quickly jumped in to give him some guidance. "But... Mr. Brown found her body that night – out in the harbor – during the Aurora Borealis..."

Randolph raised his eyebrows, but did not turn his gaze from the sunset. "Yes... Yes, that's true... She *was* gone..." He paused as a tear visibly rolls down his cheek, opening his mouth as if to suck in more air. "I didn't believe it... I didn't know Sam had..." he paused and shook his head, screwing up his face as if the words in his were vile to the taste, "... *fished* her out of the bay..." He paused again and closed his eyes. When he opened them, he turned to look at David. "I didn't know..." his voice trailed off. "It was a mistake..."

Thirty-nine

July 14, 1960

Nearly two weeks had passed since the accident. Twelve days, actually. Twelve endless days that just seemed to roll straight through twelve tear stained nights; everything suspended; everyone waiting...

And what were they waiting for? Unreasoned hope against hope held that they might yet find her, clinging to a rock or stranded on one of the many tiny little uninhabited islands in the bay; or that she had perhaps been rescued in the thick fog by one of the many Summer sailors cruising through the unfamiliar area on that fateful day, and that she was safe somewhere, but not reaching out to them because she was somehow suffering from a temporary form of amnesia.

These theories and more were championed by Randolph, who was relentless in his fierce determination to find her alive. He would not believe the worst, let alone even think it.

Claire and Randy were both devastated but struggled valiantly to remain positive; afraid, really, not to be hopeful, yet, at the same time, absolutely terrified that the absolute worst had already happened. Their age difference evaporated, somehow, as their mutual fears were communicated between themselves in wordless looks and silent tears. They had to, they knew, keep up a united facade of hopefulness for their father's sake, and so they had to wait and hope, together and alone.

And now she was alone. Randy had gone to Camden

A. Gardner Strong

with the Copelands, on the last boat, glad to get away, if only for two days, from the intensity of his father's fruitless search. He had, to his credit, checked with his sister to make sure she would be O.K. if he took a break, and Claire was certain that he would have stayed if she had asked him to.

Now she sat sadly at her mother's antique dressing table, in the Master bedroom at Sunnyside, trying to feel her mother's spirit. With the utmost love of a daughter for a mother, she tenderly regarded her mother's picture, then carefully began touching her mother's hair brush... touching her mother's string of pearls...

Claire picked up the hair brush and slowly pulled it through her long dark hair. Lifting her chin high, and drawing a deep breath, she pulled her hair back and fastened it in a clumsy bun, securing it with two of her mother's long ivory hair sticks.

She looked in the mirror and saw shades of her mother looking back, tears filling her sad eyes. She picked up the pearls and held them at her neckline, just as her mother would have done any time she was undecided about what to wear to dinner. The cotton tank top didn't frame it quite right, but she could see beyond that small detail. Claire struggled with the clasp of the necklace, watching her reflection in the mirror as tear drops rolled down her angelic face.

~

It had been a beautiful day, if somewhat subdued for the Brown family. For the past two weeks, Samuel had done his best to calmly balance the chores around Sunnyside and the farm with his employer's new urgent set of needs, wondering how long it would be before he capitulated to good, sound reason and accepted the reality of the situation. She was gone, pure and simple. Yet the man carried on like he still had a chance to save her.

Maybe Randy would be able to talk some sense into him when he got back from the mainland. Randy knew; he was sure of that. If not him, it would have to be Elsie's firm hand on the rudder, and Samuel for one would very much prefer it not be her task to set the man straight. Not that Randolph would be one to shoot the messenger, but you never knew.

He had, by consequence of all the hoopla, gotten a late start tending his traps this evening. He had missed it altogether the last several days, and much of the previous week, so he was bound and determined to at least get in one good haul this week. It was Thursday already, and he knew that Friday would be a late day at the farm, then the weekend would be upon him again, and he'd be into next week before he could get back out on the Elsie Mae. There was money in those waters, and it would have been sinful to ignore it, not with utility bills and such going up all the time.

John was becoming a first rate stern man, but he had wanted to play in the basketball game on South Island, and Samuel felt he had to indulge him, knowing that he had been leaning on him pretty hard these past couple of weeks. And so it was that he alone manned the lobster boat bearing his wife's given name, as it bobbed in the waters at the outer part of Pulpit Harbor, racing to beat the dark that was bound to close in all too soon, after which he would have no choice but to head back to shore. Samuel dropped anchor quickly and got ready to haul his line of pot traps.

~

Claire stood up and went over to her parent's bed, her mother's pearls now hanging naturally around her slender neck. Her mother had carefully laid out her dress on the bed, and it lay there still, undisturbed by her husband, waiting for Isabella to return home from her boating excursion and dress for dinner.

Claire touched the dress, a simple cotton scoop neck frock, perfect for a hot July evening. With the utmost care, she lifted it up and held it to her chest, wishing desperately that her mother would come back home and put it on.

As if possessed, Claire slowly pulled off her tank top and dropped her shorts to the floor, letting them fall in a lump around her ankles. She then slipped her arms into the bodice of the delicate cotton garment. The hem of her mother's dress fell to cover her youthful legs, then she swirled to look at her mother in the mirror.

~

Samuel had emptied and quickly re-baited only a half dozen traps before he ran into a problem. The line seemed hopelessly tangled, and he could not quite make out why as he struggled to haul it into the boat. There was no visible sign of someone else's gear having been dropped on top of his own, but he supposed some lines could have been cut loose and drifted his way.

Samuel swore under his breath in great frustration as

he strained to haul in the next trap, but suddenly realized in horror that what appeared to be a woman's hand seemed to be tangled in the line as he pulled it up out of the water and into the boat.

At that very moment, vibrant colors seemed to rise up from the waters, creating an eerie, rippling glow all around the boat. Samuel looked around, shocked in equal parts by the appearance of the body part and the unbelievable totality of what he quickly deduced must be the Northern Lights. He shivered, the timing and scope of the phenomenon being just about the spookiest thing he had ever experienced, then he hastened to continue his struggle to haul in the line.

~

Claire was standing in the Master bedroom, looking sadly into the full length mirror, when her attention was drawn to the windows as the sky transitioned from rich, dark blue into vast rippling waves of vibrant colors. She moved over to the French doors to get a better view, fearing for a moment, with almost childlike wonder, that she was witnessing the end of the world.

~

The rippling colors of the Aurora Borealis filled three hundred and sixty degrees of the sky and the waters, surrounding and isolating the Elsie Mae as if it were a planet unto itself. After great effort, keeping his wits well about him, Samuel Brown successfully hauled the body into the boat, snarled hopelessly with the seventh trap. He parted the tangled lines and saw Isabella's swollen face emerge from a matted mess of dark hair. It was as he expected, yet he moved back from the body quickly, consternation and repulsion evident in equal parts on his weathered face.

~

Wearing her mother's dinner dress and string of pearls, Claire threw open the French doors and rushed outside, frightened and completely in awe of the great, unearthly beauty of the Aurora Borealis.

Wandering slowly into the garden, Claire looked around as if in a daze. In every direction, waves of pastel color rippled upward. A part of her brain believed it knew what was happening, yet there was fear in her eyes as she looked about uncomprehending, feeling as though she had been cast into a twilight zone, completely cut off from reality. She felt overwhelmed by the vastness of the astounding event and was nearly crushed by an equally vivid sense of isolation.

Randolph suddenly came rushing into the garden, an unnaturally broad smile on his face and an almost crazed look in his eyes. "Isabella!" he cried out. "You came back! I *knew* you would come back to me!"

Claire cringed, not recognizing the look in her father's eyes. "What's happening?"

"Isabella!" Randolph cried again, not hearing Claire's question. "Thank God!" He grabbed Claire and started kissing her passionately. Claire struggled against the embrace but was clearly overpowered.

"Daddy! No!" she struggled to say, but her words were smothered and distorted.

"Isabella!" he murmured as if in a rapture, sweeping

her off her feet and carrying her back toward the open French doors as spectacular waves of color continued to ripple up through the sky.

Forty

December 15, 2006

"**C**an you understand?" Randolph cried plaintively. "I... I was so distraught – so filled with grief – All I knew was that I saw my Isabella! I *wanted* to see her, standing there in the garden! I didn't realize... until it was too late!"

David shook his head in stunned disbelief. He understood all too clearly, on an intellectual level, the full meaning of what his grandfather had just revealed. How many times in the last few weeks, after all, had he looked up at the sound of a foot fall, fully expecting that his mother might walk through the doorway, her brilliant smile leading the way? And how often had he opened the mudroom door, hoping to find her Jaguar parked safely in the garage? Yes, he understood with profound clarity the ability to believe the possibility of the absolutely impossible, but he now fought off accepting this new, fantastic account with his entire being. "You thought she was her *mother*?" he cried, incredulous.

"I was... *hysterical* with grief! Can't you understand? I would *never* hurt my little Claire! I... I just wanted her back! I *wanted* Isabella to be alive! Can't you see? I was not in my right mind!"

"How could that *happen*?" David demanded, fending off understanding, even as the truth struck him like a full body blow.

"I don't know…"

"You don't *know*?!!" David exploded. "How could you *not* know?!!"

Randolph lowered his head, tears rolling down his cheeks, his trembling hands clasped as if in prayer. "It was… a… mistake… a *tragic* mistake!"

Shaken, David had returned to his seat on the sofa, at a right angle to Randolph, his ashen face distorted by his profound shock. He shook his head and leaned forward. "*You* did it?" He stood up again slowly, not waiting for a response, his head still shaking. "*You…* you *forced* yourself on my mother?" He took a step back, awkwardly, as if pushed away by an invisible force field, his face contorted as he struggled to get his mouth to release his words. "Douglas Brown is *your* son?"

David heard a gasping sound and turned around quickly to see Elsie standing there, a stricken look in her eyes, holding onto Douglas, both hands firmly on his arm, as if to hold back the smoldering fury revealed on his face. David was stunned.

"It *was* you!" Elsie gasped.

"So… She *wasn't* lying!" Douglas proclaimed, his eyes gleaming and face flush with anger as he pulled Elsie's hands off his arm and moved slowly toward Randolph.

"My God!" Elsie cried, "He *did* see it! Old Hiram tried to tell me before he died, but I put it off to a weak mind…"

David staggered back, shaking his head in disbelief, groping for a handhold as much as for a way to comprehend the scene unfolding before him. "*You? How did you...*"

"Douglas... Please! I..." Elsie made a feeble attempt to stop Douglas from advancing on Randolph.

"No..." Douglas shouted, shaking his head, oblivious to everyone in the room aside from the aging patriarch. "No... She... She *told* me it wasn't her choice... She *told* me! *All* my life! My *whole* life! Something just didn't *feel* right... I *knew* I didn't *belong*! Like I was some kind of *alien...*"

Douglas stopped moving, fixing his glare completely on Randolph. "Who made you God?" he spat, leaning forward and pointing a shaky hand at his prey. "Who gave *you* the right to play with other people's *lives*?"

Randolph turned his head away and looked sadly out the window as the sunset faded into darkness, tears streaming down his face. He offered no immediate response, but his whole body started to tremble.

Douglas squinted his eyes, taking another step forward. "I remember you..." he said, focused on Randolph's averted face. "When I was a little boy... So *cold* and superior..."

Elsie had moved closer to David, and reached out to him for support. "Douglas... *Please!*" she cried.

"It's O.K., Ma..." Douglas finally acknowledged, then he turned and looked directly at Elsie, tears filling his eyes. "Ma... You *knew* this *all* these years? You *knew* this when I told you I didn't think Dad loved me?"

Elsie shook her head and reached out toward Douglas. "No! He *loves* you, son... I told you! He... He just shows it in different ways... We *both* love you!"

Douglas stepped back, a little unsteady on his feet. He reached out and grabbed the back of a chair to help him regain his balance. "You *knew* this when I *confided* in you that I couldn't understand why Dad favored John so much? I tried so *hard* to get his approval..."

"You don't understand!" Elsie cried. "Please listen! I... I *promised!*"

Douglas shook his head and turned back around to look at Randolph. "*Two* fathers... and *neither* one of you could manage to show me any love..."

The obvious pain in this exchange caused something to snap in David's mind and he came back to his senses. "*Doug!*" he cried out, trying, to no avail, to draw his attention from his frail grandfather and the now weeping Elsie.

"That's not true!" Elsie cried out to suddenly deaf ears. "You don't understand!"

Randolph was now regarding his son, his expression enigmatic but his eyes filled with tears. "I'm so... so... sorry..."

"You're *sorry*?" Douglas cried. "That's all you can say?"

Randolph drew a soggy breath and pulled his trembling torso somewhat erect using the arms of his chair. "What would you have me say?" he asked, looking directly into Douglas' eyes.

"*Doug!* Let's talk…" David said, feeling compelled to reach out once more to this familiar stranger who's life was now permanently intertwined with his own.

Douglas heard nothing, his focus was so completely fixed on Randolph. "Tell me *why! Why* did this happen? *Why* did you *shop* me off to your caretakers like I was some kind of *farm* animal? *Why* was I so *dispensable*?"

Randolph pushed himself up just a bit straighter, his shoulders rotating back ever so slightly as his sad eyes continued to lock on Doug's stony glare. "I couldn't have you *ruin* my daughter's life," he said, his voice even, his cadence deliberate.

"*You* didn't want *me* to ruin her life?" Douglas asked in disbelief. "Apparently *you* had a hand in that!"

David tried again, a bit more forcefully, "*Doug!* We need to talk!"

"*Yes,*" Randolph said with a sigh, oblivious to everyone but Doug, a hint of resignation clear in his face and the subtle slump of his shoulders, "And I did everything I could to *fix* it."

"Fix it? *Fix* it?!!!" Douglas exploded. "*This* is how you *fixed* it? You… You put all the burden on *these* people…" he gestured wildly in Elsie's direction. "You… You *distance* yourself and… and set *everyone* else up to *fail!*" Douglas snarled, moving to close the distance between himself and Randolph, his attention riveted on his face. "You had no right…"

And then time stopped, even as events unfolded with the swiftness and precision of the downward swing of an axe.

In his anger, focused so intently on his father, Douglas failed to notice the furniture placement as he advanced. Stepping forward this last time, his foot caught on the blanket that had partially slipped onto the floor from Randolph's lap. His equilibrium failed him, his condition being weakened as it was, and he pitched forward clumsily, colliding forcefully with the ottoman. Shocked by his unfamiliar and utter lack of coordination, he grasped blindly at the side table, instinctively trying to break his fall.

Randolph's legs were simultaneously jerked roughly to the left, causing him to lurch forward, his arms flailing out defensively. The side table wobbled, tipping just enough to send the tea cup crashing to the floor, but as the tea pot tumbled off the table, it struck the arm of the chair, promptly spilling much of the remaining hot tea directly into Randolph's lap.

Randolph cried out in pain as he wretched back in the chair, trying to throw off the blanket which had trapped the hot liquid. Douglas grabbed at the arms of Randolph's chair, trying to steady himself, but he managed only to push the chair away, tipping Randolph over backwards, into the window.

Momentarily stunned, David then tried to quickly separate himself from Elsie without hurting her. "Grandfather!" David called out, striding toward the old man. While he suffered no close personal attachment to the man, and was utterly repulsed by what he had just learned, he felt compelled to try and help Randolph, who was now crumpled against the wall.

"Douglas!" Elsie cried, moving quickly to her fallen son and extending her hand as he struggled to pick himself up off the floor.

"Wait!" Douglas protested, directing his attention toward Randolph. "I didn't mean to..."

Randolph cried out weakly, "Help me!"

"I'm sorry!" Douglas implored, looking now at Elsie. "I..."

David stepped over the tangled furniture and squatted down, gently sliding his arm under his grandfather's head, assessing the damage before he tried to lift him. His eyes were glazed, and his head was bleeding, apparently from the impact against the window. David turned his head and locked eyes with Douglas for a minute. "He's *ninety-two*, for God's sake! Whatever else he is, you need to remember that!"

"I'm sorry!" Douglas protested. "It was an accident!"

"Like my mother?" David demanded sharply.

Douglas was rocked back, stunned, realizing for the first time who David must be. David shook his head as he stripped off his shirt, then turned back to Randolph, gathering him up tenderly, just enough to elevate his head. He dabbed at the blood, then pressed his shirt firmly against the scalp wound. "Grandfather?"

Randolph tried hard to focus on his grandson. "It... It should have been *me* on that boat..." he whispered.

"It's O.K., Grandfather..."

"No, I... I went to the golf course instead," he tried to explain. "I *changed* the plan..."

"We can talk about that later..."

Randolph looked sorrowfully at David, tears flowing freely down his face, then he tilted back his head and his eyes looked straight up, as if toward heaven. "I'm *sorry* Isabella!" he proclaimed. Randolph gasped suddenly, eyes open wide, his hand moving weakly to his chest. "My heart is broken!" he croaked, his voice barely audible.

"Get his pills!" Elsie cried.

Randolph closed his eyes. "No..." He slumped as David looked to Elsie for help. "I'm sorry..." hung in the air as his last breath expired.

Forty-one

David woke up, feeling dreadfully alone and unsure, for a few fuzzy minutes, as to his whereabouts or the time and day. Blinking his eyes, the fog slowly dissipated, and he realized he was, in fact, in the bedroom of the old farmhouse. Looking around, he found the sheets and blanket were twisted and in complete disarray, confirming that he had been restless during his troubled dissent into slumber. Minutes? Hours? He had no idea. David looked toward the window, but remained in his bed, breathing deeply. His face was puffy, the flesh around his eyes a mottled rose, as he fought back a new round of tears.

The call to his father had been long and difficult; exhausting for both father and son. David had discovered, quite by accident, that his cell phone worked well up on the hill, so he had driven up there and parked next to the 1941 Chevy pick-up, leaving the motor running to hold the cold night at bay while he talked with his father.

David had been as measured as possible in his explanations, but it had been a lot for his father to process over the phone. On the one hand, his faith in his wife had been clearly vindicated; She had, indeed, not been having some kind of lurid affair behind his back. Not that Peter had ever believed any of the hurtful things that had been fodder for the local gossip mill since the accident, but it was a load lifted off his mind to have proof that his belief in his wife had been justified.

This relief, however, paled in comparison to the deep sadness he felt upon realizing the fullness of the burden she had carried alone, all these years. Had she not trusted him? Was she protecting her father? Claire had not kept a diary – at least as far as anyone knew – so there would be no easy revelation of her state of mind. It was with a heavy heart that Peter had to accept the probability that he would never know for certain why she had not confided in him, her husband of nearly thirty years, before she revealed the truth to her first born, unleashing the cork so violently from a brew too long fermented.

What had he done or said to make her choose that course? How had he made her feel that he might not be compassionate and understanding? That he would not support and protect her? If only Claire had told him first, their lives would not have been torn apart so tragically; Of this Peter was absolutely certain, and this certainty left him racked with guilt.

To complicate things further, Peter felt clearly humbled by the fact that he had not been more supportive of his son. Sure: he had humored him, letting him take on the project in Maine, but it had not been because he had believed his son's time and energy were being thereby well spent. His acquiescence had been driven more by his inability to come up with a better plan or, more to the point, a convincing argument that David should drop his quest for understanding his mother's death and go back to school.

In any event, he would most likely be flying in late Saturday or early on Sunday morning, giving himself some time to help David sort though things before the funeral.

David replayed his conversation with his father in his mind, sorry that he had not been able to have it face to face, but knowing he had done the right thing. He rubbed his forehead with his hands, then rolled over, away from the window, pulling the covers up.

~

Claire sat in the passenger seat, an uncertain smile on her beautiful face. She was looking at the driver, Doug, his hands gripping the steering wheel, and an angry, troubled look on his face. "I don't understand why you are telling me this!" he shouted, taking his eyes off the road as he glared at her.

Claire looked shocked and dismayed. "I'm sorry!" she cried. "I thought you'd be happy…"

"Happy?!!" Douglas exclaimed in disbelief, not letting her finish her sentence. "I don't believe this! You thought I'd be happy to know my whole *life* was a *mistake*? Is this your idea of a sick joke?"

His angry words hung in the air as the needle on the speedometer climbed steadily without his apparent notice.

~

David woke up, again, this time with a start. Throwing back the bed coverings, he got up and crossed to the bedroom window. Looking out, across the salt pond, his gaze wandered slowly up the path toward Sunnyside, so enchanting in the moonlight.

He could see her there. He could clearly see her rising early every morning to marvel at the unique beauty of each new day, gazing at all manner of sunrise, from magnificent to meek, through the ethereal island mist known only to those of her persuasion. Each day was new, especially for those who made the effort to wait quietly for the beauty of her arrival.

He hoped with every fiber of his being that she had watched the sunrise that fateful day in November while she pondered the step she was about to take. He hoped it had been breathtaking. Looking over at Sunnyside in the delicate light before dawn, holding this thought, David felt a tremendous sense of peace wash over him; a strange sense of comfort, surpassing all understanding.

Epilogue

December 17, 2006

David poured three large cups of coffee. He put the covers on the first two, then hesitated, staring at the third cup. After a moment, he looked over at Angela, who was behind the counter, keeping a quiet watch. "How does he take his coffee?" David asked.

"A little half & half..." Angela replied without skipping a beat.

David poured half & half into the open cup of coffee and put the cover on, making sure it was sealed tightly. Attention to detail. It was getting him from one minute to the next. He looked up and locked eyes with Angela.

She had come to the farmhouse yesterday, like an angel of mercy, with a large coffee and a fresh blueberry muffin. He hadn't felt much like seeing anyone, so when he had finally hauled himself out of bed, he had put the new little tea kettle on the old wood cook stove and settled for instant coffee and a bowl of Grape Nuts. He was surprised to see Angela at the door, but he had let her come in.

They had talked a little about his meeting with the plumber and his mothers plans to restore the old farmhouse, but they had quickly, if somewhat awkwardly, moved on to the most recent developments that had touched both their lives.

He had been honest. It impacted her and, most especially, Olivia, so he decided she really should know. He didn't think Elsie would approve, but carefully guarding the truth obviously hadn't kept everyone safe, he had reasoned. Angela had promised discretion, and he believed he could trust her.

"Pretty strange…" David murmured.

"I know…" She took his money and handed him back the change. "Everything all set for tomorrow?"

"His instructions were pretty specific," David said, dropping the change in the tip cup, "and he'd already made most of the arrangements in Rockland, so there wasn't really that much to do."

There was an awkward silence. Angela looked down for a moment, then directly at David. "I… I'm sorry about your grandfather…"

"Thank you…"

"Doug is really sorry…"

"Will you guys get back together?" David asked tenuously, ignoring her last statement for now.

Angela shook her head and shrugged. "I… I don't know… He has to figure out who he really is… and… and then we'll see…"

David took a deep breath but said nothing.

Angela broke the uneasy silence. "I… I don't know what else to say…"

"It's O.K... It was an accident..." David said softly.

Angela shook her head. "Hard to figure..."

~

David left the store, carrying a small cardboard tray with his trio of hot coffee cups, and got into his car. Angela stood by the window and watched him drive out of the parking lot, turning left, as if to head back along the winding coastal road to the farmhouse and Sunnyside, but she saw him take a quick right turn into the Fuller Cemetery.

The Winthrop family plot was easy to locate, the earth having been freshly opened behind the massive marble monument. Elsie had observed how fortunate it was that the early Winter had been so mild, otherwise the interment could not have happened in such an expeditious manner. It was common practice, she had explained, to have such events held over, in favor of the warmer days of late Spring, just so long as the business could be taken care of before the Summer Residents started migrating their way, overwhelming the ferry service.

It was unusual, David was certain, to have so much green grass leading up to Christmas on the island, but snow was, in fact, predicted. Not tomorrow, thankfully, or the next day, but it would be a white holiday without a doubt, assuming you believed the weather men in Portland and Bangor. David had seriously considered spending the holiday here on the island, but had ultimately decided that he would follow his father to New York to spend a quiet couple of days in the apartment on Central Park West. Maybe they would catch a few shows on and off Broadway. Maybe take in all the shows at Lincoln Center. They had always done the family holiday gatherings in Westport or Connecticut, so New York was clearly the best choice for this year's non celebration, especially since Amie would not be coming back from Europe just yet. It would be a difficult time – even without all these new complications — but he and his father would face it together. They would be fine.

But first there was this to contend with. Tomorrow morning, the hearse would arrive on the first boat. It would go directly to the cemetery, the casket would be lowered, the island minister would take just enough time off from his job reading the island's electric meters to say a few appropriate words, and, after the funeral director had gone back to the ferry terminal, in plenty of time to catch the middle boat, and David's father had flown back to Boston and on to New York, the local groundskeepers would fill the gaping hole with the dirt that sat there, now carefully covered by a dark green carpet. Simple; Dust to dust.

Not so simple, though, to figure out how to feel about the departed, let alone eulogize the man. It would be private, so neither David or his father would have to say much more than "Thank you" to the minister, let alone be put on the spot to say something in praise of this man, or to reflect on their loss. How could you mourn the loss of someone you never really knew? Something you never really had?

How to feel? It had been two days and it was still murky, at best. It was difficult not to sit in judgment; No, *impossible* not to sit in judgment.

How could he ignore what had happened to his mother? It was a terrible wrong. However, he believed the facts as presented: that it was a one-time event; a dreadful case of mistaken identity perpetrated by a man whose thinking was addled by extreme exhaustion and grief. While it made David wonder about the often unbridled male response to emotional triggers, he did not suspect that a long-term systematic abuse had occurred in this case.

Looking back with a critical eye over all his time he had spent with his mother, he could find no evidence that she presented in any way the kind of extensive damage that he was certain abused children must suffer. Even so, his grandfather's transgression had been illegal, and the harm ran deep and wide. He had never faced the legal consequence for his misdeed, but his punishment had been far greater, David was certain, than anything the law would have imposed.

Pity, perhaps. Yes, his anger had given way to something else; maybe he felt pity.

Whether by his design or, most likely, that of his daughter's, Randolph Winthrop had never had more than a peripheral relationship with the Winslow family. Sure, there had been birthday checks and that sort of thing, but that was it.

Mother had, David was guessing, kept her father at arm's length all these years not because she thought he would harm her children – for he was certain that was not an issue – but because she had always carried her heart on her sleeve and she must have felt that she had to protect herself from exposure to those complex and heartbreaking feelings that the sight of her father had surely triggered.

He would never know for sure, but, upon reflection, David was inclined to believe that his mother would have felt guilty about her part in the tragic unfolding of events that night in 1960. If she had not tried to capture her mother's essence by putting on her dress and pearls and pulling back her hair, she would not have induced her half-crazed father to do what he did. One could hold that there was merit to that argument, even though it truly wasn't her fault. Guilty or not, David could clearly see his mother holding it that way. In her eyes, she would have been at least as responsible as her father was, and for that she would have felt great guilt.

And then there was the whole matter of the baby; Doug Brown. How she must have tormented herself over the decision to give him to Elsie. Grandfather was clearly the architect of that "solution" but his mother had supported it for all these years, nurturing it as her father had envisioned it, right up until that final day.

Two people racked with guilt about their individual and collective choices, the consequences of which were so intricately entwined; the regrets palpable. Had they talked about the island and all that had passed on those infrequent occasions when she had gone to Boston to have lunch with him? His mother had always been respectful regarding her father, and David was sure, now, that she must have loved him deeply to keep his secret all those years, even from Elsie. It all made perfect sense, now that he knew the salient facts.

No, David didn't hate his grandfather, but he didn't feel "love" for him either, and that was an acceptable way to feel on this cold December morning.

David took a deep breath and let out a long low sigh. Understanding brought a certain level of peace; that

A. Gardner Strong

much was certain. But it was not without its costs or complications. The family tree had been severely shaken, and the irreparable consequences were dramatic; The path uncharted. Where would they all go from here?

Doug had been raised a Brown, and Elsie had been a loving mother, without a doubt. But he was a Winthrop, any way you sliced it. Should he change his name? And what about Angela and Olivia? The Winthrop name carried implications, both real and imagined; Should they adopt Doug's rightful name as well? Were they both entitled, even if Doug and Angela failed to reconcile?

And what about the farmhouse? Should he press on with his newly devised arrangement with Angela and Olivia, regardless of Doug's involvement – or lack thereof? And if Doug objected, should David defer solely to his opinion?

David shook his head as if to stop thinking – at least until his father arrived. But there was so much to consider! There would probably be issues with his grandfather's will now, given that Doug was not so much as mentioned, but David would wait for his father's input, in spite of being named, to his great amazement, sole executor of his grandfather's estate.

But then there was the still the matter of his mother's accident and the law. Should Doug face the legal consequences of his recklessness? Driving to endanger, death resulting? Did the extenuating circumstances justify forgiveness? A week ago, he would have been on the phone to Chief Macomber before Doug had uttered a second word. Now David was ambivalent; Perhaps he was still in shock. Quite beyond his comprehension, he felt a strange willing to put his hands behind his back, so to speak, and let things evolve in a more organic manner.

This last month had certainly not been a cakewalk for Doug. It was too soon to tell for sure, but David thought it likely that the anger he saw in Doug would soon give way to a profound sense of loss and personal guilt. Where his grandfather's personal torment had left off, Doug's surely must have begun. David could well imagine the mental and emotional gymnastics his half-brother must now be engaged in, grappling with the unarguable fact that he had had a hand, to one degree or another, in the death of both his natural mother and father.

David looked up when he heard the faint sound of a small plane as it circled slowly above, preparing to land on the grassy air strip just beyond the cemetery wall, in a clearing lined by tall evergreen trees.

Looking down as the plane banked slowly, Peter could see Claire's island clearly, isolated in it's natural beauty, surrounded by the cold blue waters of the Atlantic that rarely, if ever, gave back those whose souls they had claimed.

A Few Facts to Keep in Mind about the Aurora Borealis

The solar cycle lasts about 11 years and 2012 and 2013 are expected to be banner years for seeing Auroral activity.

The cover image of the Aurora Borealis by Michael Leonard was taken in Cumberland, Maine, around the peak of the last solar cycle in November, 2003.

While the Northern Lights (or Southern Lights) may seem ethereal to the viewer, the phenomenon is not without the potential to usher in a lot of real havoc!

These discharges from the sun, also called sun spots, can adversely affect and disrupt communications on earth, including wireless phone systems, short-wave radio, GPS, and satellites, and electrical grids can go offline causing sudden blackouts. In addition, there is a real risk of X-radiation exposure for people aboard aircraft flying at high altitudes.

Island Secrets

Reading Group Guide

1.   Some people who witnessed the unexpected, spectacular phenomenon of the Aurora Borealis on North Island felt as if they had somehow been temporarily propelled into a Twilight zone. Have you ever experienced a naturally occurring phenomenon that took your breath away or had an out-of-this-world feeling? Can you see how such an event might conspire with other elements to distort reality?

2.   It is clear that David Winslow was raised by two solid, involved parents, both able to offer the advantages of old money. David is responsible, well grounded, and inspired to have a meaningful life. His younger sister, Amie, is similarly purpose driven. Some families are not so lucky. What do you see as the most important element in raising children well? Does privilege blunt the emotional impact of tragic loss or does it simply ease the physical, financial, and legal burdens?

3.   The lives of David and all of the Winslow family members are catapulted into a period of intense grief and confusion when Claire is killed in the violent single car crash of her prized classic Jaguar. Peter and Amie throw themselves back into their work, but David feels angry and cheated, and is obsessed with the missing details. He wants his mother back and finds himself looking for her to walk through the door, even while he realizes it is not possible. Have you ever had to deal with the sudden loss of a parent, spouse, or child? How does the unexpected nature of the loss make a difference, in your opinion?

4. David was living in Manhattan on September 11, 2001. He was scheduled to interview for an internship at Cantor Fitzgerald later that morning, but, instead, he stood on the roof of his apartment building and watched the World Trade Center towers fall. Do you know anyone who was in Manhattan on and/or deeply affected by 9/11? How much did David's experience on 9/11 intensify his reaction to his mother's sudden death? Do you think his vivid recollections of that stunning event will continue to affect him in the future?

5. Claire had been an active volunteer at the local church and for many good causes in the town, and was much loved and respected, but some of the widespread gossip in the aftermath of the accident casts Claire as a "compulsive do-gooder" who thought she could get away with having an illicit romantic involvement with the handsome, but much younger man she had recently "taken under her wing". Why do you think people are often subject to greater, more disparaging criticism, facts aside, when they have been held up as a model of virtue?

6. Eighty-five year old Elsie, a lifelong inhabitant of the island, has been an employee of the Winthrop family since her marriage to Samuel Brown in 1942, when she moved into the old Brown family homestead, then owned by John Winthrop. Do you think that the next generation of islanders has the same sense of responsibility, belonging, and purpose? Do you think that social changes within an island population are unique or a microcosm of broader societal trends?

7. Elsie, a loyal, hard working employee, has for years put the needs of the Winthrop family ahead of almost everything. Do you think she was motivated by the

fact that (a.) this was her job, (b.) that she felt "like family" and was thus naturally protective, or (c.) that her strong Yankee work ethic and reserve made her the perfect employee?

8. We know that Claire has always had a kind heart, as seen in her youthful exchange with Uncle Chester. Do you think her lifelong volunteerism and bent for helping others was a core attribute or was she driven by a perceived need to make amends?

9. Uncle Chester is fifty-six years old, but can not read or write, and has limited cognitive skills. He is well cared for and works hard along with his older brother, Hiram, doing exactly as he was told, though not always happily. Claire has a strong sense that Uncle Chester must be very lonely in his protected little universe, especially during the long off season when she wasn't around. Would his life have been significantly improved if he had been born even fifty years later? Training him to be a productive family member, contributing to the operation and maintenance of the farm, did Hiram essentially provide him the vocational training that is an integral component of current practices applied to working with the developmentally disabled?

10. Hiram moved back to the island from Boston to take care of his mother and brother when he came back to pay off his father's debts and to settle his father's estate and, much like George Bailey, discovered that his younger brother had been offered a good job in Augusta, working for his fiancée's father. Being a farmer had not been part of his dream, but he became resigned to the fact that it was obviously his destiny. Do you think Hiram felt he had no choice but to shoulder the responsibility because he was the eldest

son? Has society moved us beyond this ethic or is this still a viable model for today?

11. Hiram's father, Samuel, had tended him through the night when he was seventeen and delirious with fever, saving his life but falling deathly ill two days later. Do you think Hiram felt responsible for his father's death? How did this affect his decision to return to the island to care for his mother and brother?

12. Hiram's wife, Elisa, drowned in the Mill Stream during a stormy full moon tide, the desperate act of a deeply depressed woman. Hiram had not understood her lack of happiness and tender enthusiasm for her first born, and was completely bewildered by what he perceived as his wife's sullen resentment of him and their child. Though he knew better, Hiram maintained her drowning was an accident, determined to protect his wife's reputation because she had not taken his son with her into the rushing waters. Postpartum depression was an unknown diagnosis in 1917. How did women cope with profound depression years ago? Under the circumstances, was there anything that could have been done to help Elisa? What advances have been made in this area? What more can be done?

13. David is plagued by recurring vivid nightmares about his mother's last moments, all variations of her possible reaction to the impending crash. Do you think they are triggered by the fact that David just couldn't understand why a virtual stranger (to him) was allowed to drive her precious Jaguar in such a reckless manner, or was it just an extreme manifestation of his reaction to the fact that he had no opportunity to say good-by to his beloved mother? Is he angry with his mother?

14. David stumbles upon some evidence which suggests his mother had some secret business up in Maine, but as he is drawn deeper into the mystery surrounding her connection to Doug, he initially refrains from sharing too much information with his father. He is clearly trying to protect his father from some potentially painful truth. Do you think he was right to handle it this way? Should he have ignored the gossip and simply shared his father's blind faith in his mother?

15. Consumed by his deep sense of loss and lack of closure, David puts his education on hold, against his father's advice, and sets out to immerse himself in his mother's past on the island, hoping to find a way to truly understand the circumstances of her death, as well as deal with his unremitting anger toward the man who took her from him. Have you ever known someone to become obsessed with and, to some extent, take on the life of a dead parent? Why do people deal with such loss in widely disparate ways?

16. Doug's coma and grim prognosis resulted in legal inertia for a time after the accident. David is angry and anxious to have the full force of the law make Doug pay for what he considers, at best, negligent homicide. Do you understand how David feels when he has a better understanding of the facts? What do you think will or should happen?

17. On the island, David learns the details of his grandmother's death in a tragic boating accident, forty-six years ago, and finds that she is buried on the island, next to her son who was later killed in a helicopter crash in Vietnam. His mother has been back to the island only once since her mother's death, and David's maternal grandfather – the fragile, ninety-two year

old Randolph Winthrop, with whom he has had a respectful but perfunctory relationship for his whole life — still owns the property across the pond from his mother's antique farmhouse, though he too has been absent from the island for many years. Did Claire love her father? What is the primary reason that Claire keep her father at arm's length for so many years? What is the primary reason that Randolph accepted such a minor role in his daughter's and grandchildren's lives? In the end, what is Randolph's biggest regret?

18. By chance, David discovers some startling secrets, long concealed and jealously guarded, which have almost incomprehensible ramifications. In an explosive confrontation with his grandfather, he uncovers the truth about an unthinkable crime and is left to grapple with some unpleasant facts, as well as the many far-reaching, unintended consequences of well intended choices, all aimed at protecting Claire — and those she loved. How do you view the events of July, 1960, in terms of right and wrong, good and bad? Is it black and white or gray and entirely understandable? Who is most accountable for what happened in this unfortunate chain of events? Are the consequences, immediate and over time, equal to or greater than the crime?

19. *Island Secrets* is set entirely in New England, yet it speaks to several universal themes, with strong, authentic characters of both genders and across several generational bounds. How does this story make you think about the virtues and the pitfalls of "managing the truth"? Can you think of any situations in which you might apply such reasoning? What lessons can be learned?

20. Beyond the story, there are implications of many far-reaching, unintended consequences of well intended choices which resulted in blurred genealogical lines for more than one generation. Thinking about Doug, Angela, and Olivia, do you see any issues that may be relevant, in any way, to the now broad practice of artificial insemination, anonymous sperm donation, surrogacy, and, potentially, cloning? How does this differ from issues arising from traditional adoption? How important is it for children to know who their genetic parents are? Is the impact on the children quantifiable and real or undefined and psychological?